THE INHERITOR

THE INHERITOR

≒ A PLAY ≓

COLLECTIVE CREATION OF THE THÉÂTRE DE L'AQUARIUM (1968)

Translated from the French by Kate Bredeson and Thalia Wolff

NORTHWESTERN UNIVERSITY PRESS

EVANSTON, ILLINOIS

Northwestern University Press
www.nupress.northwestern.edu

The play is freely adapted from the book *Les héritiers: les étudiants et la culture* (Paris: Les Éditions de Minuit, 1964), by Pierre Bourdieu and Jean-Claude Passeron, in which the two sociologists showed that success at school was above all determined by matters of cultural heritage and social class.

Printed in the United States of America

10 9 8 7 6 5 4 3 2 1

LIBRARY OF CONGRESS
CATALOGING-IN-PUBLICATION DATA

Names: Théâtre de l'Aquarium (Paris, France), author. | Bredeson, Kate, translator. | Wolff, Thalia, translator.
Title: The inheritor : a play / collective creation of the Théâtre de l'Aquarium (1968) ; translated from the French by Kate Bredeson and Thalia Wolff.
Other titles: Héritier. English
Description: Evanston, Illinois : Northwestern University Press, 2024.
Identifiers: LCCN 2024024916 | ISBN 9780810147829 (paperback) | ISBN 9780810147836 (ebook)
Subjects: LCSH: College students—France—Paris—Drama. | Education, Higher—Social aspects—France—Drama. | Social classes—France—Drama. | LCGFT: Drama.
Classification: LCC PQ2680.H414 H4713 2024 | DDC 842.914—dc23
LC record available at https://lccn.loc.gov/2024024916

CONTENTS

ACKNOWLEDGMENTS

The Ruby-Lankford Grant for Faculty-Student Research at Reed College gave us the support to start this project. We appreciate the Undergraduate Research Committee—and Jolie Griffin in particular for outstanding administrative support—for evaluating our proposal and awarding us this grant.

We are grateful to the acting company who collaborated on a staged reading of the first draft of this translation on October 11, 2021, in the third-floor atrium of Reed College's Performing Arts Building. Thank you AJ Adler, Leo Barnes, Emma Campbell, Maya Dearman, Isaac Ellingson, Naama Friedman, Hannah Danaë Goodman, Leo James, John Mark Poole, Hailey M. Poutiatine, Odilon Rojas, Azure Sensabaugh, Sizheng Song, Marco Andrés Tonda Keller, Juniper White, and Daniel Yogi, for helping us hear the translation aloud for the first time, for bringing your energy and commitment to this work, and for showing us how *The Inheritor* matters to you. Thank you to the Reed Theatre Department—Barbie Wu, Kate Duffly, Peter Ksander, Rusty Tennant, Alissa Warren, and Charlie Wilcox—for your support of this event and our project.

We offer our abundant gratitude to Joelle Rameau, for your meticulous work collaborating with us on complicated questions about translating phrases and larger cultural contexts. Your expertise in both languages, as well as in the French educational system, helped shape this translation.

Thank you to Wendy Weckwerth for your work in editing, proofing, and fact-checking. Your sharp eyes and attention to detail make our writing shine.

We are grateful to Marisa Siegel at Northwestern University Press for enthusiastic support of this project and for giving this play a home in the English language. Thank you to Courtney Smotherman for your work to obtain the rights. We appreciate the efforts of Isabelle Alliel at Actes Sud for helping with translation rights.

Thank you to Fanny Abib-Rozenberg and Rosine Evans for feedback on early stages of this translation. Merci à Pierre Fortier for vocabulary assistance.

Kate's thanks include: In Paris, the library staff at the École normale supérieure and the Bibliothèque Gaston Baty for help with early work on this play. A Fulbright Scholarship initially brought me to Paris and made the early parts of this research possible, and I remain grateful to the Fulbright Commission, Amy Tondu, and Arnaud Roujou de Boubée. Thanks to Catherine Faggiano at the current Théâtre de l'Aquarium, and the staff at the Bibliothèque nationale de France Richelieu's Arts du spectacle department. Thank you to Yale University's Department of French for sending me on exchange to the École normale supérieure in 2003–4, an experience that paved the way to me finding this play. Later, Reed College's Stillman Drake Funds and Summer Scholarship Funds provided research support related to this project; I appreciate the Reed Dean of Faculty for awarding these funds to support my research. Victoria Fortuna, Simone Waller, and Marisa Plasencia's generous feedback influenced this work. Thank you to Loghaven Artist Residency, where I finished the final editing of this manuscript. Thank you to Aaron C. Thomas for your friendship, your expertise in close reading, and your ever-present enthusiasm for helping think through questions about writing. I am grateful to Lindsay Brandon-Hunter, Michelle Liu Carriger, Jessica Del Vecchio, Jacob Gallagher-Ross, Chloe Johnston, Patrick McKelvey, Shayoni Mitra, Noe Montez, Cindy Rosenthal, and Donovan Sherman for your support, advice, care, and wit. Thank you to my family of Fohrs, Garreltses, Huths, Bredesons, and my dear Tennessee (*toujours*) for support past and ongoing. My friend family around the world sustains me, and I am grateful in particular for Derek Applewhite, Kris Cohen, Miriam Felton-Dansky, Danielle Berger Fortier, Julie Fry, Allie Hankins, Josh Miles, Margot Minardi, Karima Ridgley, and Lauren Tompkins. I thank my teachers, especially Beth Cleary, Elinor Fuchs, Peter Rachleff, Joe

Roach, Marc Robinson, and Catherine Sheehy, for the sparks you lit. Thank you to my students past, present, and future: this play helps us in our ongoing questioning of academia from the inside.

Thalia wishes to thank: Sizheng Song and Bridget Perier for bringing our staged reading of *The Inheritor* into archival life through, respectively, your program and photography; the activist student communities at Reed College, Emerson College, and beyond for your dedication to changing the world for the better through your action and discourse; my French teachers, Ann Delehanty, Chris Higashi, Luc Monnin, Deirdre Sennott, and Catherine Witt; my family, Kris and Kat and Claire and Juniper Wolff, for their support, patience, curiosity, and willingness to indulge lengthy intellectual discussions; my English teacher Rebecca Tresch; Lynn Galletta and the teachers and students at Galletta School of Dance, who taught me the value of community, mind-body connection, and joyful art-making; Jacqueline Levenseller, who inspired me to become a theater educator and continuously reflect on best practices in both theater-making and educating; Grace Camp, Lizzy Cooper Davis, Rivka Eckert, Audrey Johnson, Jenn London, Tiffany Maltos, Johamy Morales, AmyLynne Murr, Bethany Nelson, Cassie Post, Julianne Shea, Joshua Rashon Streeter, Gabi Tatone, Mike Thomas, and countless others for supporting that mission; and Katia Queener for love and support during the writing process and beyond.

INTRODUCTION

Kate Bredeson

The Inheritor, a play collectively written in spring 1968 by a group of students at the elite École normale supérieure (ENS) in Paris, unflinchingly portrays the lives of two university students. One grew up with money, weekend visits to museums, and family members with experience in higher education. The other had a contrasting experience, with a childhood marked by scarcity and after-school jobs. The play juxtaposes the two students—called the Inheritor and the Non-Inheritor, respectively—as they embark on a period of cramming for a university exam that will determine their futures. With unapologetic didacticism and cutting absurdism, the play stages the two students alongside one another, mired in their proficiency and lack thereof, alongside a cast of professors and family members.

The exam at the center of this play is not a regular class test; it is an elite university entrance exam with exceptionally high stakes. Both students' futures are dependent on the outcome of this exam. If the Non-Inheritor passes, he will be catapulted into a different, previously unattainable social class—that of the Inheritor. In the Anglophone world, this would be akin to, upon passing the exam, emerging with the standing of someone from Oxford, Cambridge, Harvard, or Yale. Within the French educational system, to pass this exam means entering the specialized top-tier system of what is known as the *grandes écoles*. The writers of this play—who themselves were from the ENS, France's most prestigious institution of higher education—drew on their own experiences within this system to create this heightened, high-stakes world.

The results of the exam are anticipated from the beginning: the Inheritor succeeds, while the Non-Inheritor fails. Yet the journey is still harrowing. The play ends with a direct challenge to the audience:

applaud the end of the performance, and you too are complicit in this system. *The Inheritor*, which debuted at the ENS on May 3, 1968, at the very beginning of the countrywide strikes and shutdowns that would become known as May '68, is as relevant in 2024 as it was more than fifty years ago, even in a different language and cultural context. As higher education in English-speaking countries grows increasingly expensive, student debt becomes more punishing, and teaching institutions expose their corporate perspectives, the play will only grow in its crucial and topical significance. This is especially true in the wake of the 2023 Supreme Court decision to strike down race-based affirmative action. This is why I wanted to make this play accessible to Anglophone students, teachers, directors, actors, readers, and audiences.

From the start I wanted to translate the play with the help of a student. After all, *The Inheritor* is by, about, and primarily for students. Its subject felt particularly timely when I started this translation project in the 2020–21 academic year. It was a moment marked by the COVID-19 pandemic, of course, but also by a rise in student activism on college and university campuses in North America in response to Derek Chauvin's murder of George Floyd in Minneapolis. An eruption of protests called for police abolition and racial justice in summer and fall 2020, and these calls are ongoing. At the same time, labor-related protests swept France in spring 2021—incorporating a wave of occupations of theaters as ideal places to enact utopian dream spaces, just as in May '68. As I write this introduction in spring 2023, youth in France vociferously participate in and lead protests against President Emmanuel Macron's use of Article 49.3 of the French Constitution to push through a change in retirement age from sixty-two to sixty-four years old. While the events of 1968 during which *The Inheritor* premiered and those of 2020–23 were more than half a century apart, they share deep resonances and fierce urgency as collective calls for systemic change. With all of these factors at work, it felt right to return to this play at this time.

In winter 2021, I approached my student Thalia Wolff, who also speaks French and was then a junior at Reed College, where I teach, about working with me on this translation. We started our translation process in late spring 2021 and had an early draft ready for fall 2021. Wolff directed that draft as a staged reading, cast with students. After the reading, the students onstage and those in the audience expressed unanimously engaged responses, commenting, "This play is about us," "When will it be published so we can do a full production?" and "We need this play—now." The staged reading participants were a mix of students—Inheritors and Non-Inheritors. Some were first-generation college students coming from low socioeconomic means. Others hailed from great privilege. All were studying and working together on an elite liberal arts campus that mirrors the university portrayed in *The Inheritor*.

The student company's enthusiasm for the play prompted us to continue working on translation and partner with Northwestern to publish it for English-language speakers to read, study, and perform. *The Inheritor* is about education access and inequality. It speaks to faculty, staff, families, and most of all students in and around our institutions of higher education. It should be read, studied, and produced. As the student writers of *The Inheritor* reflect in the play, we are all complicit. Staging this play opens a necessary conversation and inspires us to do better.

The Play

I first encountered *The Inheritor* in the third volume of Robert Abirached's terrific four-volume book *La décentralisation théâtrale (Decentralization of the Theater)*, published by Actes Sud-Papiers in 1994. I found the 2005 second printing in a bookshop across the street from the Censier campus of the Sorbonne University in Paris, where I was researching my first book in its performing arts library. The third volume, *3. 1968, le tournant (3. 1968, The Turning Point)*, focuses on theater, twentieth-century efforts by the French state to decentralize theater, and the events of 1968. This play appears in the book's appendix, accompanied by a short preface by Bernard Faivre—a member of

Théâtre de l'Aquarium until 1977, and later a theater professor at Paris Nanterre University. The themes of the play, its creation process, and the timing of its premiere made it a perfect case study for my book *Occupying the Stage: The Theater of May '68.*

In that book, I describe in detail the history of the play and its production. To understand the play's context, I offer a short summary here, drawing on information from *Occupying the Stage.* The Théâtre de l'Aquarium, a student theater troupe that started as the Théâtre 45 in 1963 and brought together students from the ENS and other Parisian universities, collectively created *The Inheritor.* The Aquarium was one of many young theater troupes that students founded and ran in the 1960s in France. Its inaugural name, Théâtre 45, comes from the address of the École normale supérieure at 45 Rue d'Ulm on the Left Bank, in the Latin Quarter. At first the young artists focused mostly on contemporary and classic plays. Then, in the mid-1960s, the company sought to create its own work. The company members chose a new name, Théâtre de l'Aquarium, an homage to the prominent fountain in the ENS courtyard, and declared in their mission, "We all work with the same spirit: not to imitate professionals but to find our own repertoire, which is new and original." The company defined its job: "to conduct the work of research" on stage.[1]

After touring various stage works to theater festivals, in 1968 they embarked on a new project, their second collective creation, with the goal of making a performance by, about, and for their peers, especially those at their mythic and prestigious institution, the ENS, where such luminaries as Jean-Paul Sartre, Marie and Pierre Curie, Michel Foucault, and Simone Weil all studied, and where Samuel Beckett taught. The ENS is an institution of deep privilege for its students, known as Normaliens. As Georges Pompidou vividly describes, "One does not become, one is born a Normalien, as one is born a knight," and "One is a Normalien as one is a blood prince."[2] I got a taste of this during 2003–4, where as a student at the ENS I observed and experienced firsthand the remarkable elitism, prestige, and privilege of the institution. Pompidou's quips highlight the class system, with the knight as a part of Old Regime aristocracy.

In their questioning of the institution from within, the Aquarium took inspiration from Pierre Bourdieu and Jean-Claude Passeron's 1964 sociology study, *Les héritiers: les étudiants et la culture* (*The Inheritors: French Students and Their Relation to Culture*), which exposes the great inequities in the French educational system and the way scholarly success in this system was more a matter of cultural and social advantage than academic growth and achievement. The 1960s saw rising frustration among French student populations about ailing infrastructures, outdated rules, imperialism, and colonialism. Students were asking piercing questions about the hierarchies and systems that ran their institutions—and society. "On the Poverty of Student Life," a student pamphlet produced by the Internationale Situationiste and students at the University of Strasbourg in 1966, became a rallying cry for the Aquarium's generation of students: "We might very well say, and no one would disagree with us, that the student is the most universally despised creature in France. . . . A modern economic system demands mass production of students who are not educated and have been rendered incapable of thinking. . . . The university has become a society for the propagation of ignorance. . . . The student is already a very bad joke."[3] This wave of questioning and dissent fueled what became known as May '68—and it echoes across the student unrest I witness as I write this over five decades later.

With the 1960s French student context and this study in mind, the Aquarium members—including Jacques Nichet, Jean-Louis Benoît, and Didier Bezace—embarked on a project to adapt the Bourdieu-Passeron study into a play. Nichet, who functioned as director, recalled, "A student troupe, playing for a student audience, we decided to play students and to direct ourselves."[4] They elected to work collectively, because collective creation—at least in theory—mirrored the breakdown of social hierarchies they sought to achieve. The group studied the Bourdieu-Passeron text and then used a four-step process to make the work: "in-depth study of the original text (group reading, discussion, research), collective writing of the basic structure, stage experimentation based on the first draft (improvisations and stage research to establish the playing style and the mise-en-scène), and then writing of the definitive draft."[5] They conducted research on their school as part of their composition process.

The result is a play that seizes on the possibility theater holds to clearly stage power relationships. The members of the Aquarium sought to create a mirror of their own world, one where everyone on stage had access to the same codes and rules, while one lone character—the Non-Inheritor—is left out due to his social class. One of the most arresting examples of this is in the play's childhood games scene: the Inheritor and the Non-Inheritor play popular children's games like the French equivalent of Simon Says, but the Non-Inheritor doesn't know the rules and becomes the object of ridicule. This scene illustrates so clearly how the play's outcome is predetermined and unmovable.

From the traditional three coups that start the play to the Greek-inspired chorus, the Aquarium's use of metatheater adds to its heightened sense of drama. Similarly, the play's reliance on absurdism only further emphasizes the bizarre nightmare world in which the Non-Inheritor finds himself. Language breaks down over the course of the play, with the powerful professors' speech devolving into babble as they give instructions to the exam. They go on to grade the exams by counting chicken eggs, where each egg becomes a winning point for one of the competitors. In this way, the exam is reduced to an elite tennis-like game that is played point by point.

At the end of the play, predictably, the Inheritor passes the exam and the Non-Inheritor fails. After the exam, the winner sings:

> *I am the phoenix*
> *I am the rare bird*
> *That you meet in every corner of the woods*
> *I sing and I die*
> *In order to sing again*
> *With a stronger voice*
>   *[Indicating* THE NON-INHERITOR*]*

You will never be reborn from your ashes
Parrot savant
Because you don't know how to sing
Like the phoenix

. . .

   [*The alarm clock from the beginning begins to sound. The*
   actor playing THE INHERITOR *comes downstage and says:*]

Thus ends our comedy
Night of insomnia, night of wakefulness
If you applaud, you will be applauding injustice
Never say "good luck"
The dice are loaded
If you applaud, you will be applauding injustice
We are all accomplices.

The play's didacticism is central to its structure and necessary for its success. Placing the Inheritor and the Non-Inheritor side by side and showing where one soars while the other falters makes the play's message starkly evident. The play's professors are all bizarre birds who flap and squawk, while other absurdist elements—a talking record player, a disembodied knight's head—showcase how out of sync higher education is with the rest of the world in this play. Didacticism in late 1960s French theater was, in part, a response to Bertolt Brecht's recent popularity on French stages. His influence resulted in an increase in didactic dramaturgy, particularly in activist plays of this period.

   The play premiered at the ENS on Friday, May 3, 1968, at the very beginning of the series of events that would become known as May '68, a period marked by student and labor protests that led to building occupations, countrywide strikes, and social and cultural upheaval that shut down much of the country from May through mid-June. The Aquarium prepared a program for the play's opening that included information about student success rates alongside quotes from Bourdieu and Passeron. While the timing of the opening with the early events

Suffit-il de constater et de déplorer l'inégale représentation des différentes classes sociales dans l'enseignement supérieur pour être quitte, une fois pour toutes, des inégalités devant l'Ecole ? Lorsqu'on dit et redit qu'il n'y a que 6 %ide fils d'ouvriers dans l'enseignement supérieur, est-ce pour en tirer la conclusion que le milieu étudiant est un milieu bourgeois ? Ou bien, en substituant au fait la protestation contre le fait, ne s'efforce-t-on pas, le plus souvent avec succès, de se persuader qu'un groupe capable de protester contre son propre privilège n'est pas un groupe privilégié ?»

P. Bourdieu et J.C. Passeron : Les Héritiers, p. 111

À ses débuts, cette troupe choisit de faire une illustration des cours de Sorbonne en montant des pièces de Marivaux et de J. J. Rousseau, puis elle eut des buts plus ambitieux : faire redécouvrir des textes trop peu connus, tels le théâtre de Mérimée en représentant «Le ciel et l'enfer», hors festival à Nancy ainsi que «Les Espagnols en Danmark». En même temps, la troupe poursuivait une animation culturelle de la Sorbonne en participant à des conférences de poètes contemporains. Elle faisait également de nombreux montages poétiques, notamment sur «La Ballade de la Geôle de Reading» d'Oscar Wilde.

Peu à peu, la troupe s'orienta vers la création de pièces inédites, pensant que cela devait être un des buts du théâtre universitaire. Elle monta aussi successivement des pièces inédites de Vera Haim, Augusto Lunel, Jeanine Worms, Pierre Gripari. Enfin, dernièrement la troupe a présenté «Le Drame des Constructeurs» de Henri Michaux, un Cabaret-théâtre Daniel Sorano

... de la Comédie Moderne de la Sorbonne présente par ailleurs ... théâtre de l'Epée de Bois, une deuxième pièce inédite de Pierre Gripari, auteur de Lieutenant Tenant, «La Damnation de Méphisto»

Chances scolaires selon l'origine sociale en 1962 (pourcentage des jeunes de 18 à 20 ans faisant des études superieures par rapport au nombre total de jeunes de 18 à 20 ans dans chaque catégorie sociale)

Salariés agricoles	0.8 %
Ouvriers	1,6 %
Professions libérales et cadres supérieurs	58,5 %

Inégale représentativité des classes sociales dans l'Université (rapport entre la part de chaque classe dans l'Université et sa part dans la population active en France)

Salariés agricoles	0,6 %	4,3 %
Ouvriers	8,4 %	36,7 %
Professions libérales et cadres supérieurs	28,5 %	4,0 %

Cette inégalité de représentation est-elle due à une infériorité congénitale de talent ou de capacité de travail chez les classes sociales les plus défavorisées ? Evidemment non :

Pourcentage des étudiants de chaque catégorie ayant réussi à leurs examens - avec une mention - avec deux mentions :

Etudiants des «hautes classes»	39 %	18 %
Etudiants des «basses classes»	58 %	33,5 %

Cela signifie que les fils des classes sociales défavorisées qui arrivent à entrer à l'Université réussissent mieux que les autres. En d'autres termes, pour ces étudiants, l'accès à l'Université n'est dû qu'à des aptitudes particulières, qui ne sont pas indispensables à l'accès des fils des «hautes classes».

Figure 1. Pages from the original 1968 program of *L'héritier ou les étudiants pipés* by the Théâtre de l'Aquarium. The program features information about student access and equity in France at the time.

of May '68 was coincidental, the play's focus on themes that would be central to the May student protests is remarkable.

The production played a second day on May 4, but after that it was no longer possible to continue as planned due to the protests. Given the play's topicality, the Aquarium decided to take their production on a local tour to striking schools around Paris and its suburbs. The play required no substantial adjustments in light of the May events, though in several scenes the company changed the professors' costumes to those of baton-carrying CRS state riot police. On May 17, *L'Humanité* critic Philippe Madral, who saw the production in Châtillon-sous-Bagneux, wrote: "The result is remarkable. Avoiding all the traps of document-theater and 'agit-prop,' the Aquarium collective, under the leadership of their driving force, Jacques Michet [*sic*], has succeeded in writing a play of great political scope, and also a rare funniness, that at this present moment constitutes a study which has been perfectly adapted to the day-to-day rapid evolution of the student revolt." The next day, Jacques Lanval wrote in *La Réforme*, "The coincidence with the news is fortuitous, but how very powerful."[6]

After successful stagings around Paris, including at the occupied École des Beaux-Arts, the company eventually stopped performing the play. Faivre remembers: "In the exaltation/disorganization of May '68, to organize or even simply get the troupe together was an impossible mission. And, in the following months, it seemed more important to us to produce other plays instead of again taking up *L'héritier*, which seemed out of date in our eyes thanks to the student revolt."[7] *L'héritier* left lasting imprints on the company. Nichet noted that after May '68, "we abandoned story, plot and psychology. . . . Our theater was transformed by the use of documentary material; we no longer used the stage as a place to celebrate eternal cultural values, but as an instrument for elucidating social issues, and as a form of group expression."[8] Judith Graves Miller notes one impact of the production: "The play also provided a degree of catharsis for the student strikers who saw it during May '68. . . . This experience and the total impact of the May movement encouraged the troupe to renew its political commitment and reconsider its student position."[9]

Though I quote short passages from the play in *Occupying the Stage*, until now the full play has been inaccessible to Anglophone readers. Given that the play provides both a dazzling example of what I call the Theater of May '68 and a crystalline portrait of education access and inequality that—as my students attest—resonates deeply today, I wanted to bring it to the attention of English-language readers, directors, students, and audiences. During the staged reading process, Wolff and I found that *The Inheritor*'s didacticism invited our company members and our spectators to try to think, feel, and act in service of improving our education system from within, particularly by demanding change from those in power. Defining, even for oneself, who is an Inheritor or a Non-Inheritor provides meaningful opportunities to reflect on privilege on and off campus. The play asks contemporary students to grapple with inheritance, succession, and the reproduction of roles in the social and political hierarchies of late-stage capitalism.

The Translation Process

The process of translating this play started as I worked on *Occupying the Stage*. I translated sections of it for my second chapter, "Social Relations on and off Stage: Revolutions of the Théâtre du Soleil and the Théâtre de l'Aquarium." In that chapter, I discuss changes in working methods for some French theater artists during the 1960s as they sought to mirror the social transformations they sought outside the theater in their creation and production processes. For that chapter, I translated three passages from the play, including the closing monologue to the audience, as well as multiple excerpts of lines. As I do in all of my translation work, I consulted a French colleague, in this case Joelle Rameau, to verify and help me hone my translations.

Then, in late 2020, I approached Wolff about assisting me with this translation. It was crucial to me—given the subject matter—that I work with a student who was immersed in the issues present in the play. At this early stage, I also wanted Wolff's perspective on whether current students might see themselves in *The Inheritor* and whether the play even made sense to translate. I had another May '68 play in mind if this one didn't feel relevant. After early conversations, and Wolff's enthusiastic response to the play's topicality, we applied to a summer fund at our institution for faculty-student research in the humanities. With the support of the Ruby-Lankford Grant for Faculty-Student Research, Wolff and I spent summer 2021 working on a first draft of our translation.

After reading and discussing the play, studying translation theory, and discussing together the historical context of the play and the Theater of May '68, Wolff entered the French text into a shared document, creating a column on the right to enter, line by line, our English translations. In the English column, we each worked in a different font color, so the author of the different lines and parts was clear. We gravitated toward different sections. (I was excited to work on the Louvre picnic scene, while Wolff wanted to translate the exam section, for example.) We worked on some passages together, and we reviewed and edited each other's work. We expanded our team by inviting former Reed language scholar Fanny Abib-Rozenberg, who is Parisian, to be our summer 2021 language consultant. Wolff regularly spoke with her to review questions and notes. We kept a separate running document where we compiled ideas, quandaries, and questions to discuss together. Our typical working style was to work on the translations separately, and then meet to discuss our efforts.

One of our earliest questions was about the title. The French title, *L'héritier ou les étudiants pipés*, doesn't easily translate. *Étudiants pipés* literally means "the loaded students," in the same sense of "loaded" as in the term "loaded dice": the outcome of a roll is fixed ahead of time. This was tricky, since in English "loaded" is common slang for "drunk," and that meaning would surely supplant the other connotation. When discussing the play in my first book, I translated its title as *The Inheritor, or the Privileged Students* to center the idea of a predetermined outcome. In the absence of a more appealing alternative, we decided to keep that title translation. However, the French holders of the rights to the English translation stipulated that the English title should be just *The Inheritor*, and I liked how the shortened title felt crisp, bold, and direct. When I later worked on a major revision to our translation, I elected to use the word "chance" in lieu of "opportunity" throughout, as in lines like "Because the exam is the first and last chance that I'm being given" in order to evoke the sense of the game that the original title offers.

Another exciting challenge was translating the passages with rhymes. The play features many sections that use rhyme, alongside passages with no rhyme. We kept rhyming passages when they appeared this way in the original. Our general approach was, when necessary, to slightly alter the original meaning of individual words to achieve the rhyme in our translation. For example, not all of the birds in the avian rhyme section match up exactly with the French birds;

instead we prioritized creative solutions to maintain both the bird references and the rhyme. We found the beat scheme and cadence important to how the passages propelled the action forward and created an intense, rhythmic sensation of anxiety for the Non-Inheritor.

We also discussed gender in the play. In French, both the Inheritor and the Non-Inheritor are called "he." We wondered about this, particularly given the large population of trans and nonbinary students on our campus, and especially in the theater department. Would they see themselves reflected in a play that called the main characters "he"? Abib-Rozenberg pointed out the sexism of 1960s French student culture, and how this is reflected in the play. Wolff noted the gendered ways both the lead characters act with their families and fellow students. We ultimately decided to keep both as "he," given that we also maintain the 1968 and French settings, with the understanding that any student of any identity could play both of these characters.

We had a parallel conversation about race and religion. The race of the students is not stated, though it is implied throughout that both the Inheritor and Non-Inheritor are white. There is one explicit mention of race in the play, during the *Jacques a dit* game, where the Seventh Student says "La lessive ne peut blanchir un nègre." In a literal translation, this is "Detergent cannot bleach a Negro." We first chose to translate this as: "Detergent can't change the color of one's skin," which renders the intent of the line but omits the word "Negro." However, for our final draft we returned to the more literal translation. This choice felt important to reflect the play's cultural context—1960s, post–Algerian War Paris. Further, keeping the line as written highlights the racist foundations of contemporary elite educational institutions on both sides of the Atlantic, and how racism, even today, contributes to ideas of who is and is not an Inheritor. For similar reasons about past and present French history, we kept as is the reference to the yellow star and the ghetto, in which the Seventh Student rallies other Inheritors by borrowing this imagery and evoking France's long virulent antisemitism and the country as a site of the Holocaust. We note too that observant Jews could not take the ENS entrance exam because these were always held on the Sabbath, and the institution did not make religious exceptions. In both the bleach line and the yellow star moment in the play, the Aquarium writers purposefully evoke the racist and antisemitic underpinnings of French higher education and society as a way to further extend their scathing critique.

While we discussed moving the setting from France to the U.S., we decided not to do so, as the play is uniquely French, though the points it makes have a wide reach. We kept some references as in the original, such as the mentions of Charlemagne and Jules Ferry. We did, however, translate some other references (ones that are not the names of prominent people) into ones better known in English, and in some cases we slightly adjusted references to make them make sense in English. The children's game *Jacques a dit* became Simon Says, which offers a close analogue. Uses of the verb *"agréger"*—which reflects a French idiomatic phrase for passing the competitive *agrégation* exam—prompted us to focus on the competition aspect in our translation. Any student who completes their studies graduates, but only a select few become *agrégés* in a particular discipline. So we translated the play's opening "Reçu, accepté, agrégé" as "competed, admitted, accepted" to highlight the order of the process and amplify the competition aspect. Some terms caused us particular vexation, especially "le petit polar," which is used several times. French colleague Joelle Rameau helped us discover that this word corresponds roughly to the idea of a "nobody"—in the case of an unpopular student who is ostracized for not partying, not belonging to any clubs, and for focusing instead on studying. She suggested that we try the word "traitor," which is what we decided to use, and we think it is fitting given the context of the Inheritor from the in-group and the Non-Inheritor from the out-group.

After helping me with a few translation passages for *Occupying the Stage*, Rameau joined this project toward the end of the process. French and bilingual, she served as a final set of eyes to help us refine and expand our choices. I worked with her as a consultant on the final two drafts of the translation, which I significantly revised from the manuscript Wolff used in the staged reading. In addition to her excellent notes about specific vocabulary choices, Rameau amplified a crucial larger point about the French higher education system, in which she both studied and has taught—she and I met in 2004–5 when we were both teaching in the same high school. Some of the language in the original play highlights the relationship between the French educational system and religion. Indeed, the whole setup of the play mixes religion and education, when right at the beginning the Bird-Bailiff proclaims:

> Hell and damnation
> Death and resurrection
> The first will be the last
> The last will be the first
> Ignore the distinctions on this earth
> Your happiness is beyond
> Ignore the privileged by birth
> And God will reward you before long
> Outside the Church, there is no salvation
> The Church chooses the chosen.

From the start, the world of *The Inheritor* is one where religion and education mingle, and where advancement in education is "rewarded" by God. References to heaven and hell abound. When the Second Ancestor announces, "I am your uncle, the rector, and I am opening the doors of heaven for you," the connection between educational access and a pathway to heaven is glaring, even as practiced in a contradictory fashion.

All of this speaks to the long-standing relationship called *laïcité* in French, most often translated as "secularism." Karina Piser defines *laïcité* as "the legally enshrined secularism that has formed the backbone of French social and political culture since 1905. *Laïcité* goes beyond the U.S. interpretation of separation of church and state in an attempt to create an almost post-religious society." It is an idealistic and uneasy relationship, where in theory French schools support the separation of church and state, and yet this doesn't always play out so clearly. I saw this firsthand while teaching high school English outside of Paris, during the same year that France banned religious symbols in schools. What this meant at the school where I worked was that when I taught "English" lessons about holidays—which was part of my teaching assignment as the imported English speaker—I was reprimanded for "promoting a Jewish agenda" while talking about Hanukkah, but was directed to speak about Christmas because this was a "cultural holiday" and "not a religious one." While religious symbols had been banned by the government, a Christmas tree sat in a public hallway. In theory *laïcité* is an Enlightenment ideal to protect the rights of individuals, but in recent decades it has been wielded as a way to persecute Muslims, Jews, and others who practice religions outside of Christianity. In the original French version of *The Inheritor*, the reference to French statesman and philosopher Jules Ferry (1832–1893) is a nod to the laws that carry his name, which established free and compulsory secular public education. This highlights how *laïcité*, even as practiced and enforced in contradiction, is a pillar of French education.

One other conundrum in the play that caused vexation is the stage direction right before the final monologue: *"The alarm clock from the beginning begins to sound."* And yet in the published version of the French play, there is no mention of an alarm at the beginning. However, in the original 1968 typescript of the play, which is in the Arts du spectacle department at the Bibliothèque nationale de France in Paris, I noticed that there is a stage direction at the very beginning in which the Non-Inheritor enters the stage, turns on a desk lamp, and sets the alarm clock. We elected to restore this stage direction for our translation, in part because it helps explain the presence of the alarm at the end of the play, as well as increases the sense of stakes throughout, and establishes that the play is a fever dream that takes place over the course of a night of last-minute studying. While there are other differences between the original script and the published French one, overall we drew our translation from the published French script. Additionally, we added a character list and several stage directions to help a reader envision the play in production.

Throughout the many drafts of the play, I noticed that the absurdism in *The Inheritor* is pronounced; *The Inheritor* premiered eighteen years after Eugène Ionesco's *The Bald Soprano* opened in Paris, so the evolution of the absurd makes sense. Indeed, the absurdism in the play demonstrates how well this playwriting style works to convey a sense of an out-of-sync world of nightmares and anxiety. While some scenes—the vocal exercises, the Louvre picnic, the exam—are relatively clear and recognizable in terms of the action being presented, there are others that are notably wild. The VistaVision film passage and the knight's head scene are among the most bizarre. The dramaturgy and language of these scenes feature fractured, exaggerated, and sometimes out-of-place language as a way to amplify the nightmarish world in which the Non-Inheritor finds himself in this level of higher education where the cards are stacked against him from the beginning. The play's use of absurdism drives home its point: that the world of higher education is unclear and impenetrable for those who don't possess the secret language and inherited codes to access it. In this world, academia feels and looks like a haunted house with overstated characters and violence. The stakes of *The Inheritor* are as high as possible: the Non-Inheritor must crack the code or, as his mother says, "If he fails, he will always remain the same. There, that's all." It was an exciting challenge to work with the authors' original language to try to capture the same sense of anxiety and inequality that is core to the Aquarium's imperative. Suzan-Lori Parks writes that "content determines form and form determines content."[10] The Aquarium writers composed *The Inheritor* as a piece of didactic absurdism because this was the best way to convey the story of education inequality and access in France in the 1960s, and this holds as true today.

This translation of *The Inheritor* is a part of my larger goal: to research theater as a tool for radical activism. It also stems from my great investment in French activism, and especially French theater, and my desire to bring these extraordinary aspects of French culture to English-speaking readers and audiences. Theater and activism have long been linked in seismic ways in France. In translating this play with Thalia Wolff, I seek to bring the play and its moment in theater history to Anglophone students, teachers, families, directors, and readers to share a part of the dazzling history of May '68—and to inspire activism in schools, institutions, and streets today. *The Inheritor* offers a striking example of how theater can play a vital part in activist work.

NOTES

1. Kate Bredeson, *Occupying the Stage: The Theater of May '68.* (Evanston, IL: Northwestern University Press, 2018), 85.
2. Bredeson, *Occupying the Stage*, 85.
3. *Occupying the Stage*, 86.
4. *Occupying the Stage*, 86.
5. *Occupying the Stage*, 86.
6. *Occupying the Stage*, 91.
7. *Occupying the Stage*, 91.
8. *Occupying the Stage*, 91.
9. *Occupying the Stage*, 91.
10. Suzan-Lori Parks, "Elements of Style," *The America Play and Other Works* (New York: TCG, 1995), 7.

REFLECTIONS ON THE STAGED READING AND COMMUNITY DISCUSSIONS OF *THE INHERITOR*

Thalia Wolff

When Kate Bredeson approached me with the opportunity to help translate a play exploring pressing questions about education access and equity, I was excited to discover this devised script from 1968. I was also interested to explore the Bourdieu and Passeron sociological text from which the student devisers derived their inspiration. In reading these works for the first time, I was struck by how relevant the challenges they raise remain. Still today we engage in a shared pretense of equality of opportunity in higher education. The challenges *The Inheritor* raises to this presumption felt like pressing concerns while my peers and I were enmeshed, and to varying degrees implicated, in this imperfect system of higher education as students at Reed College, which describes itself as "devoted to the intrinsic value of intellectual pursuit and governed by the highest standards of scholarly practice, critical thought, and creativity."[1] The project also spoke to important, and challenging, considerations for a campus like Reed's, which encompasses an energetic student-activist population. Like many college and university students, Reed students engage in protests, outreach, and systems of mutual aid, both within and outside of the college, advocating for improved conditions. During my time at Reed, students actively fought for issues like affordable meal plans, divestment from banks financing prisons and fossil fuel industries, youth voter activism in relation to climate change, Black Lives Matter, and community safety reform. As I participated in these campus conversations and studied theater, I became interested in the ways theater could be a part of protest and activist projects on and off campus.

What interested me most about how the Aquarium troupe adapted Bourdieu and Passeron's ideas about education for the stage was how they actively grappled with their own positionality as students attending an elite institution of higher education. In applying the sociologists' concepts to their own lived experiences—and the embodied medium of performance—the students had to consider what it meant to be implicated in and benefitting from, even as they sought to resist, a system that perpetuated inequality of access and outcomes. I was also struck by the script's theatricality. Its description of a nightmarescape featuring a floating head, bizarre avian educators, and a runaway chorus of Inheritors and ancestors demands to be staged. This is a theatrical and movement-driven text—and I was inspired to put it before an audience, bringing renewed life to the Aquarium's brilliant work and inviting discussion of its ideas within and outside our campus community. I was elated, then, to direct a public staged reading of an early draft of Bredeson's and my translation of *The Inheritor* in October 2021. Our short rehearsal process emphasized collaborative and spontaneous creation. We hoped to provoke the Reed community into an active discussion and conscientious consideration of the play's ideas about educational access and how members of a college community may be implicated in the institution's dysfunction.

I sourced participants for the staged reading from the Reed College student community through a variety of channels, including a departmental email list for students interested in theater projects, as well as personal outreach, both to those with whom I had worked before, and to those I knew had interest in the topics and themes under consideration. In addition, professors in the French, English, and theater departments agreed to ask their students if they might be interested in participating in the reading. The result was a group of seventeen students who varied in academic background, interests, and experience, but shared an interest in the topic at hand. We were all inherently connected to the structures explored in the play through our enrollment at Reed. In our staged reading of the then in-process translation, the emphasis was on bringing the words and themes of *The Inheritor* to life. Because we were interested in the impact the play would have on a college community, we wanted to make sure it could be presented in front of an audience, and that both readers and audience were invited into an in-depth discussion of the play's themes and content.

One challenge in bringing the words of the play to life was casting. This surreal and metatheatrical play's characters aren't always clear; some are combined, some speak in the play-within-the-play as part of the Chorus of Inheritors, some are nonhuman objects like the record player. Further, even as clashes in generation, authority level, and class persist, boundaries between characters who fulfill similar roles fluctuate: ancestors, family members, and Inheritors blend together, all taking part in the same sinister games. Key examples include the Inheritor's farce about the life of the Non-Inheritor, in which the Inheritor and his classmates produce a crudely rhymed play depicting the Non-Inheritor and his family, as well as the Inheritor's "best day of vacation" sequence, in which the Inheritor's family members are simultaneously figures in the story he is writing and supervisors of the writing of that story. They comment on the action and structure of the play within the play's narration at the same time that they actively participate in its unfolding. Two notable exceptions to this murkiness of character distinction are the Bird-Professors, who are frequently distinct from and at times in opposition to the students; and the Non-Inheritor, whom the text sets in clear and perpetual contrast to the Inheritor and his chorus. Before casting the reading, I created a character list and figured out where roles could be double- or triple-cast, and what kinds of doubling made dramaturgical sense. This informed the cast of characters that we have listed at the top of the play.

Pandemic conditions limited the scope of possible casting interpretations for this reading. The number of named characters suggests a large number of reading parts, but COVID-19 restrictions in Oregon in fall 2021 required that, even masked, the number of performers should be limited. In light of these logistical and safety constraints—and considering how characters comment on and blend into one another—I elected to take an alternate casting approach. The Chorus of Inheritors and the group of Bird-Professors each encompassed readers of two, three, and sometimes more speaking parts within the constraints of their assigned category. The Inheritor and Non-Inheritor were the only two roles without doubling because they are present in and critical to almost every scene of the play.

Bredeson and I originally envisioned the staged reading as a simple event. The rehearsal would be a chance for the readers to become familiar with the text, structure, and ideas of the play. The performance would involve minimal staging, but would mostly be an opportunity for the audience to hear the play and engage in a community talkback. While the discussion and talkback elements were maintained, the rehearsal process evolved as it became evident the complicated text and multiple double-castings required a more involved staging.

I adopted a collaborative and spontaneous creation process for the reading, encouraging everyone to find their own meaning in their lines as they read through and spoke the text, but also to speak up whenever they had a question or idea about how to better understand or more effectively represent the themes being explored. In many instances, the play spurred the readers to suggest key elements of staging that enhanced the legibility of key moments in the play. For instance, the Bird-Professors originally sat with the Chorus of Inheritors, but while the play text calls for each group to speak in unison many times, one student noted that the text never has the two groups speak together, and often sets them in opposition to one another. Hence, it stood to reason that the professors needed to sit apart from the rest of the characters. Because the characters are described as Bird-Professors, the students playing them flapped their arms as they entered the stage for the first time. This movement dramatically affected how everything else felt on the stage; it evoked a chilling sense of authorities looming, or hovering, over the students as they began their predestined journeys toward the exam. While there was a door near the performance space from which the Bird-Professors could theoretically enter when needed and exit when their scenes were done, I found it more hauntingly prescient (and the cast found it more fun) to have the Bird-Professors present onstage for the duration of the reading, perched on a conspicuous bench upstage left, where they surveyed the action from afar and occasionally squawked out an ominously approving echo of a key phrase or line being spoken onstage.

We decided to use movement patterns to emphasize the contrast between the two main characters' disparate approaches to preparing for their exam: the Non-Inheritor's position of perpetual, frantic studying, and the Inheritor's more wandering position of reminiscing, playing, slacking off, receiving advice, and generally distracting the Non-Inheritor with the weight of his noisy advantages. The Non-Inheritor remained at his desk for most of the play, except in scenes where the Inheritor was traveling with him. Meanwhile, the Inheritor has the freedom of mobility, as well as the free time, to wander around with the Chorus of Inheritors—who variously represent his privileged peers, his entitled family, his prestigious ancestors, a general group of students, and crude interpretations of the Non-Inheritor's family—at times surrounding and menacingly taunting the Non-Inheritor, skipping around him as he ducks their taunts and rhythmic gestures, trying to remain focused on his studies. The children's games scene was especially powerful when linked to the chorus's repetitious collective movement patterns around the stage, evoking a ritual of exclusion in the case of the Non-Inheritor and indoctrination to conformity in the case of the Inheritor, who is included in their games because he is family, and thus is able to learn the rules.

The inherent strangeness of this play—which includes the resurrection of a disembodied knight head, quick transitions between verse and prose, elevated diction and slang, and an abundance of absurdities and extreme juxtapositions—made our exploration of the text immersive and entertaining, without reducing the clarity of the semi-staged reading's message. In both rehearsal and performance, our process emphasized the importance of community discussions about educational access and inequality, ideas at the core of the Aquarium student troupe's play, in an attempt to bring these considerations to light for the Reed community. In both rehearsal discussions and in the community talkback, *The Inheritor* spoke to the concerns of contemporary campuses nearly as effectively as its themes spoke to 1968 France. Granted, the historical specificity of the play occasionally sets its events apart from certain features of modern campus life in the literal sense—not all readers were familiar with the particularities of Normalien campus culture, or the formal structure of French humanities essay composition, for instance. However, the allegorical and didactic nature of the play's experimental and pointed dramaturgy made its contemporary relevance unavoidably clear to readers and audiences. Throughout our exploration in rehearsal, and in watching the staged reading, I was struck by how the play's didacticism performs so well onstage in an educational environment, and many of us in the company remarked on how much we want to see—and make—a full production.

The final exam scene, where the Non-Inheritor and the Inheritor are directly juxtaposed in a televised face-off adjudicated by the three Bird-Professors, spoke to audience members and readers alike in effectively laying out the systemic unfairness of the supposedly meritocratic system of education. Several student readers discovered unfortunate parallels between their educational experiences and the Second Bird-Professor's approach—such as the self-satisfied elitism of avoiding a straightforward explanation of process, and his preference for the Inheritor's praise over the Non-Inheritor's good-faith questions about the text. The scenes with the Inheritor's family are a wake-up call to some readers about how, even as we seek to distance ourselves from the outmoded beliefs of the previous generation, inheritance can have a more insidious influence in our structures of thought than many of us would like to think.

One scene that was especially effective in sparking vibrant discussion, in both rehearsal and the audience talkback, features student protestors blocking the doors to the exam hall, passing out fliers, and declaring an end to all exams. In response to this righteous ruckus, the Non-Inheritor serves up an indignant protest of his own: "Wait until my exam is finished!" Unlike the Chorus of Inheritors, the Non-Inheritor feels he cannot afford to protest against what he believes is his best opportunity for getting ahead: his final chance at passing the competitive aggregation exam. This scene raises important questions in relation to student protest culture. In no way does the text suggest the students are wrong to rise up against an unjust system; quite the contrary, as the play was readily adapted to be performed in support of striking students at French universities. However, the Non-Inheritor's words, justifying his lack of participation in this particular demonstration, for which he is accused of being a "sellout" by his peers, demand a more active consideration of capacity and privilege in relation to student protest work:

THE NON-INHERITOR: Don't raise your hands to vote, comrades! Your soft hands will expose you!

SIXTH STUDENT: You are insulting a worker.

THE NON-INHERITOR: In short, you want to boycott luck. Because the exam is the first and last chance that I'm being given. A worker who is looking for work doesn't go on strike.

FOURTH STUDENT: The workers are inviting us to join them!

EIGHTH STUDENT: You're making a deal with the regime.

THE NON-INHERITOR: You're fascist collaborators disguised as resistance fighters. If they kick you out, you come back in through the window. I'll be tossed into the street.

Examining the role of privilege in activist work—who can afford to engage in it and who has the most to lose from fighting back against the system—spurred insightful discussion among community members during the talkback. Reed students, professors, and other community members considered together how questions of access and inequality could affect the distribution and dynamics of power inside movements of resistance against oppressive systems. Echoes of these conversations returned in the organization of student protests, including walkouts and a building occupation, in spring 2022 in response to a community instance of hate speech. The Aquarium's nuanced observations in *The Inheritor* remain relevant to present-day narratives of revolt and resistance.

THE INHERITOR

Collective Creation of the Théâtre de l'Aquarium (1968)

Translated by Kate Bredeson and Thalia Wolff

Figure 2. Sizheng Song's poster and program design for *The Inheritor* at Reed College.

The final speech of the play, sung by the Inheritor, directly confronts audiences and readers with their potential complicity in the systems that perpetuate educational inequality: "If you applaud, you are applauding injustice. We are all accomplices." In the public staged reading, this line led to considerable hesitation and visible discomfort on behalf of many audience members. One spectator attested to not being certain what to do in this moment; he wanted to celebrate the readers' and translators' work, but he didn't want to endorse unjust systems of oppression. In rehearsal, some readers even expressed concern about this way of ending, asking, in effect: I understand the point this speech is trying to make, but in what kind of position does this place the audience, and readers? Are we supposed to just sit here in silence when the play ends? How do we signal that the reading is over?

In my view, the answer is that the play, and the ideas at its core, aren't concluded when the final words of the text are uttered. The concerns the play raises, and the systems and structures it challenges, surround us: we were immersed in them long before any of us encountered *The Inheritor*, and it will likely take considerable time and effort to dismantle them. The play leaves readers and audiences devoid of tidy conclusions. Instead we are offered a call to action that is simultaneously an indictment: "We are all accomplices." By acknowledging our complicity, the play invites us to move forward, asking: What can we do to make things better? I make no attempt at a broader conclusion here, but I am convinced *The Inheritor* has the potential to provoke meaningful questions, necessary discussions, and positive collective actions in the communities it reaches.

NOTES

1. "About Reed," Reed College, accessed October 13, 2023, https://www.reed.edu/about-reed/.

THE INHERITOR
Collective Creation of the Théâtre de l'Aquarium (1968)

Figure 3. Staged reading of *The Inheritor* at Reed College
on October 11, 2021.

CHARACTERS

The Non-Inheritor
The Inheritor, who also plays:
    The Intellectual Worker
    The Worker's Son
Ten Students
Eight Ancestors
Three Bird-Professors, who later become:
    President of the Jury
    First Assessor
    Second Assessor
The Secular School Teacher (played by a Student)
The Father (played by a Student)
The Non-Inheritor's Mother
The Elementary School Teacher
The Inheritor's Father
The Inheritor's Little Sister
The Inheritor's Mother
The Park Ranger
The Bird-Bailiff
The Record
The Lunch Lady
The Knight of Espine
First Proctor
Second Proctor
The Usher

Casting Note
What follows is one example of how the roles in this play can be combined to be performed by a smaller cast. This is the casting for fifteen

actors used in the staged reading directed by Thalia Wolff at Reed College in 2021.

The Non-Inheritor
The Inheritor / The Intellectual Worker / The Worker's Son

The Chorus of Inheritors:
First Student / Ancestor / The Secular School Teacher /
    The Elementary School Teacher
Second Student / Ancestor/ Another Student
Third Student / Ancestor / The Father / A Student
Fourth Student /Ancestor / The Knight of Espine
Fifth Student / Ancestor / The Inheritor's Father
Sixth Student / Ancestor / The Park Ranger
Seventh Student / Ancestor / The Inheritor's Little Sister
Eighth Student / Ancestor / The Non-Inheritor's Mother
Ninth Student / Tenth Student / The Inheritor's Mother

First Bird-Professor/ President of the Jury
Second Bird-Professor / First Assessor
Third Bird-Professor / Second Assessor
The Bird-Bailiff / The Record / The Lunch Lady / First Proctor /
    Second Proctor / The Usher

[*The stage is intentionally very simple: downstage right is a table and a chair. This is* THE NON-INHERITOR's *favorite spot, where he will spend the night cramming just before the exam. Off-center left, a bed, the favorite spot of* THE INHERITOR, *who prefers to rest—as he's always done—before the exam. The staging visibly oscillates between these two positive and negative poles: from the bed to the table, from the table to the bed. Biting and violent music, originally composed by P. E. Will, accompanies all the sung passages.*]

[*Music.*
THE NON-INHERITOR *enters.*
He turns on a desk lamp
Sets the alarm clock
Takes some pills
Gets to work . . .]

[THREE BIRD-PROFESSORS *enter and approach* THE NON-INHERITOR, *who is sleeping, and whisper—or shout—their truths into his ear. Ghostly pantomime. Death and resurrection.*]

THREE BIRD-PROFESSORS:
Segregation, integration
Segregation, integration
Ritual of initiation
Separated, detached, rejected

Competed, admitted, accepted
Competed, admitted, accepted
Admitted, accepted

THE NON-INHERITOR [*in his dream*]: Accepted . . . ?!!

THE BIRD-BAILIFF [*passing at the back of the stage*]:
Hell and damnation
Death and resurrection
The first will be the last
The last will be the first
Ignore the distinctions on this earth
Your happiness is beyond
Ignore the privileged by birth
And God will reward you before long
Outside the Church, there is no salvation
The Church chooses the chosen.

THREE BIRD-PROFESSORS:
You are the last
The last of the last

FIRST BIRD-PROFESSOR: Shoemaker, no higher than your shoe.

SECOND BIRD-PROFESSOR: Mason, stay at the bottom of the wall.
    Don't even think of the great beyond.

THIRD BIRD-PROFESSOR:
Outside of school, no salvation
School chooses the chosen.

[THREE BIRD-PROFESSORS *go out.*]

THE NON-INHERITOR: Leave me alone, I have work to do.

[*Laughter from* THE CHORUS OF INHERITORS, *all dressed in white, who suddenly enter the stage to put on the play* The Inheritor . . .]

THE INHERITOR: We, the students—we, the chosen—are honored
    to perform for you this evening the very pitiful comedy of the
    young intellectual worker.
Get ready!
We're going to get this show started.
The characters are:
His father: the mason. It's a big part!
His teacher: he doesn't talk much, but it is important!
Himself: I'll play his part! I can relate to the character.
And finally, the chorus: there always needs to be a chorus to express
    all the rest.
Get ready!

[*The curtain rises.*]

THE CHORUS OF INHERITORS:
At the very beginning was the father, a mason
Who only ever worked on commission.
He filled holes in the wall on weekdays,
And filled his belly on Sundays.
He was so happy with his only son
Who worked as an apprentice, learning construction.
Business was brisk and easy. Better than just breaking even.
They made good money in their sweet little heaven.

ALL:
But, in the shadows the education tempter
was lurking: the dismal public school teacher.

THE SECULAR SCHOOL TEACHER:
Child! Child! Listen to me and you will be happy!
Disown your father, a poor man, so shabby!
Drop the shop, start reading like there's no tomorrow
Zola, Loti, Boileau, Camus, Victor Hugo.

THE INTELLECTUAL WORKER:
Thank you, sir, thank you for granting without babble
the pleasures denied to the children of the rabble.

THE FATHER: For God's sake.

THE CHORUS OF INHERITORS:
For God's sake, said the father, irritated at his sass
throwing him out with a swift kick to the ass.

THE WORKER'S SON:
A kick in the ass hurts the conscience,
Am I a fallen angel, perverted by science?
I have to earn my bread by the sweat of my brow
A highbrow, slighted and discounted as lowbrow.

THE FATHER:
Tremble, ungrateful child! Sinful son,
punished by your sin, without grace and pardon,
be condemned, cursed, to erect fortifications
of paper and ink: nothing reliable, nothing so certain.

THE WORKER'S SON:
The hope of a sturdy wall, the hope of calluses won
pushes him to work as if under the gun!
[*To* THE NON-INHERITOR]
Hampered, panting, pressed for time, fraught,
laboring for words, laboring for naught.

THE NON-INHERITOR: Bastard! Stop your dirty comedy! You're scared
of me, you're scared of my work! Yes, long live last-minute cramming! If I'd not been burning the midnight oil, I'd long ago have
been reported missing in action. I'd be a thief if I wasn't working.
I don't work hard enough. I'd like to be able to work my way up to
the top. I want to work so I can crush you. I want to pass my exam.

[*Everyone laughs. They go out.*]

[*This parodic scene—theater within theater—is played as broad farce. In reality, it's an end-of-year student variety show. Only Inheritors have the freedom to perform with ease, and they move about casually.* THE NON-INHERITOR'S MOTHER *enters, slowly, tired. She kneels down very close to her son's table; he has started working again.*]

THE NON-INHERITOR'S MOTHER [*scrubbing the floor*]:
Don't mind me, I have work to do too.
At school, they told me they were very happy with you,
You've worked so hard so you will succeed,
Do you feel good, at least?
You shouldn't worry so much;
You failed the exam several times, and so what . . .
If you fail, what will it change?
What's the point of all of these books?
You think it'll make you happier?
You've managed to make sense of this all?
It's not healthy to stay locked up, not to see anyone.
Why don't you have any friends?
Has staying cooped up here made you sad?
You can't become a sad bore.
You don't talk to me like you used to.
You look like you're ashamed of us, like you wish you could leave us.

[THE NON-INHERITOR *doesn't even look at her. He keeps on working. She slowly withdraws.*]

THE NON-INHERITOR: I close my eyes, I dream, I dream of myself. I see myself like those who succeed without too much work. I see myself at ease, radiant, elegant, able to speak comfortably. I brilliantly hold my own, I look like I'm in the know. I stand out from the rest. I see myself . . .

THE INHERITOR: You see yourself like me.

THE NON-INHERITOR: I already told you to get the hell out of here.

THE INHERITOR: If I go away, you'll never know how to succeed.

THE NON-INHERITOR:
Yes, I will! By working, to the end!
To beat the odds! Where there's a will, there's a way!
Now, just get the hell out of here . . .

THE INHERITOR: With pleasure! And sorry for your loss at exam time
tomorrow.

THE NON-INHERITOR: I'll take it just fine without you!

THE INHERITOR: You know very well that you're going to get stuck
in the end. Everyone knows it here, and nobody gives a damn. I
heard you, I did. I'm answering your call. I was born to teach you
how to succeed.

THE NON-INHERITOR: To succeed?

THE INHERITOR: I'm going to rest a bit. Don't mind me, get to work!
I need to build up strength tonight. The race is long, you have to
get off to a good start. Don't move! I'm letting myself go. They're
going to coddle me. After that I'll feel better, I'll be able to help
you. We'll go together to the exam. I'll show you how it's done.
Good night! Get to work! I'm taking care of you, I'm being taken
care of too.

[THE ANCESTORS *enter, dressed in black, masked like corpses. They enter like children, frozen, broken, either by hopping on one foot, jump-
ing rope, or walking or playing in ways evocative of childhood, but all
in a very slow manner.*]

FIRST ANCESTOR: We, the ancestors, come to teach you how to play
and to win.

SECOND ANCESTOR [*low and rhythmically*]:
Who's going to play with us?
Who's going to play with us?

ALL [*echoing*]: Who's going to play with us?

THE INHERITOR: Play what?

THIRD ANCESTOR: Blind Man's Bluff.

THE INHERITOR: What's that?

FIRST ANCESTOR: You'll see.

[*They blindfold him.* THE INHERITOR *wanders, trying to find* THE ANCESTORS.]

THE INHERITOR: Where are you? Where are you?

FOURTH ANCESTOR: Behind you, behind you!

THE INHERITOR: Where? [*He grabs someone.*] Who is it?

SECOND ANCESTOR: I am your uncle, the rector, and I am opening the doors of heaven for you.

THE INHERITOR: Who is it?

FIRST ANCESTOR: I am your grandfather, the professor, and I am opening the doors of the schools for you.

FOURTH ANCESTOR: I am your cousin, the merchant, and I am opening the doors of the safe for you.

FIFTH ANCESTOR: Who's going to play with us?

ALL [*in unison*]: Who's going to play with us?

THE INHERITOR: Play what?

SIXTH ANCESTOR: Hopscotch!

THE INHERITOR: What's that?

SECOND ANCESTOR: It's heaven and earth.

FIFTH ANCESTOR [*singing*]: If it's heaven, keep hoping.

ALL [*rhythmically*]: If it's earth, keep suffering.

FIFTH ANCESTOR [*hops on one foot*]: Heaven! Heaven! Heaven! Heaven! [*Singing*] *If it's heaven, keep hoping.*

ALL [*rhythmically*]: If it's earth, keep suffering.

[THE INHERITOR *hops on one foot.*]

ALL: Earth, earth, earth, earth.

SEVENTH ANCESTOR: You have to know how to aim skillfully.

EIGHTH ANCESTOR: You have to know how to hop lightly.

SIXTH ANCESTOR: You have to avoid stepping on the lines, otherwise you'll need to restart.

ALL [*very low*]: Who's going to play with us?

[THE ANCESTORS *climb up on the bed.*]

THE INHERITOR: Play what?

SEVENTH ANCESTOR: Tag.

THE INHERITOR: What's that?

SEVENTH ANCESTOR: High up, sure to be saved!

SIXTH ANCESTOR: Tag, you're it!

FIFTH ANCESTOR: Tag, you're it!

THIRD ANCESTOR: Can't catch us! We are untouchables.

[THE INHERITOR *rushes to* THE NON-INHERITOR.]

ALL: No!

FOURTH ANCESTOR: Don't touch him! You must not play with a worker's son.

SECOND ANCESTOR: Who's going to play with us?

ALL [*in unison*]: Who's going to play with us?

THE INHERITOR: Play what?

FIRST ANCESTOR: Simon Says!

THE INHERITOR: What's that?

FIRST ANCESTOR: Do what you're told.

THIRD ANCESTOR: Simon says: "Smile!"

SECOND ANCESTOR: Simon says: "Put your hand in front of your mouth when you yawn."

FOURTH ANCESTOR: Simon says: "Reach your hand out and say hello."

FIRST ANCESTOR: Simon says: "Learn your lessons."

SIXTH ANCESTOR: Simon says: "Don't tell lies."

FIFTH ANCESTOR: Simon says: "Plenty is no plague."

SEVENTH ANCESTOR: Simon says: "Detergent can't bleach a Negro."

EIGHTH ANCESTOR: Simon says: "Charity begins at home."

THIRD ANCESTOR: Simon says: "Silence is silver, but speech is golden."

THE INHERITOR:
Simon says: "Speech is golden."
Simon says: "Earth is heaven."

Simon says: "High up, sure to be saved."
Simon says: "Do as you're told."

SECOND ANCESTOR: You're gifted, you'll succeed. We did it all. Play
without us, it's just a game.

[*They leave, walking at the same playful pace, in slow motion.
Enter* THE ELEMENTARY SCHOOL TEACHER, *masked.*]

THE ELEMENTARY SCHOOL TEACHER: Hello, children! Won't you say
"hello" today?

THE INHERITOR: Hello!

THE ELEMENTARY SCHOOL TEACHER: Won't you say "Hello, Madame"?

THE INHERITOR: Hello, Madame!

THE ELEMENTARY SCHOOL TEACHER: Won't you say "Hello, Madame
the head teacher"?

THE INHERITOR: Hello, Madame the head teacher!

THE ELEMENTARY SCHOOL TEACHER: Very good! You're making
progress, my little one. Continue to listen and you'll go far. You'll
become a good student. Who can tell me what a good student is?
[*Speaking to the classroom*] What did Charlemagne say when he
rewarded the poor children in the schools? He said, "Anyone can
become a good student." It's been mandatory to be a good student since Jules Ferry—the statesman who made primary education free and compulsory. Well, I can see I'll have to teach you
everything. Your education starts with me. First and foremost,
you must be masters of your sphincters, and this includes your
mouth. Let's start with the basics: the vowels. There are five vowels, as there are five aces in my deck. [*Displaying a set of enor-
mous cards, with each one representing a vowel*] Without an ace,
you can't take anything. Without vowels, you can't say anything.

Try to say "accumulator" without vowels! All that's left is teeth gnashing.
There are five vowels: A, E, I, O, U. Repeat!
Who wants to repeat? No one?

[THE INHERITOR *raises a finger.*]

Ah! Open your mouth and make an "A" sound.

THE INHERITOR [*singing in an ascending scale*]: *Ah, ah, ah, ah, ah, ah.*

THE ELEMENTARY SCHOOL TEACHER: Ah, this is wonderful! You know how to sing, you know the scales at your age. Shame on the rest of you. The youngest among you is giving you a lesson!

THE INHERITOR [*resuming triumphantly*]: *Ah, ah, ah, ah, ah, ah.*

THE ELEMENTARY SCHOOL TEACHER: He doesn't just repeat like a parrot, he's actually singing.

THE INHERITOR: *Ah, ah, ah, ah, ah, ah.*

THE ELEMENTARY SCHOOL TEACHER: Continue my darling!

THE INHERITOR: *Ah, ah, hee, hee, hu, hu.* [*Off key*] I forgot.

THE ELEMENTARY SCHOOL TEACHER: But it's quite all right, it's part of the process. Culture is what remains when you've forgotten everything else.

THE INHERITOR [*standing on the bed, singing*]:
When you have guzzled everything
Drunkenness
The stem glass
With its big stem
Better an empty bottle
Than a full bottle
When you've swallowed everything

Bountifulness
The remains remain
The snack buffet
With its big snack
Better an empty stomach
Than a full stomach
When you have forgotten everything,
Laziness
The remains remain
Culture
With its big cult
Better an empty head
Than a full head

THE ELEMENTARY SCHOOL TEACHER [*rhythmically*]:
Here are the letters of the alphabet
Here are twenty-six playing cards
Child's play,
The rules are elementary
They are learned at home, with your family.
It's by playing rummy, the easy game, first
that you train to win at poker
Who speaks, wins.
If at home, and there is a misdeal
Give up.
But if you know the tricks, the calls, the bids, the cons, the responses,
then, you scream.

THE INHERITOR [*rhythmically*]:
Show me the money!
I'm aces with the lingo
Two pair, three of a kind, full house,
flush, four of a kind, straight flush
Those who can't call are bluffed
They can't cheat.

They're pigeons.
So, they get plucked.

THE ELEMENTARY SCHOOL TEACHER:
Fair segregation.
You have to play War,
a game of cards where the kings beat the jacks
Bring down those who can't.
Those who do not know
How to play the alphabet game
Which makes or breaks kings and jacks
The rules are elementary
They are learned at home, with your family.

[THE ELEMENTARY SCHOOL TEACHER *exits.* THE INHERITOR'S FATHER, MOTHER, *and* LITTLE SISTER *enter. They stand behind* THE INHERITOR'S *bed. This is a grotesque pantomime.*]

THE INHERITOR'S FATHER: Describe one of the best vacations you ever had.

THE INHERITOR'S MOTHER: Describe one of the best vacations you ever had.

THE INHERITOR'S LITTLE SISTER: Describe one of the best vacations you ever had.

THE INHERITOR: School was out. When I woke up in the morning, I felt quite happy. We were going to have one of the greatest vacation days we've ever had.

THE INHERITOR'S FATHER: My father had decided to take us on a picnic, if I dare say so.

THE INHERITOR'S MOTHER: Mother had prepared a big basket full of treats for us to enjoy.

THE INHERITOR'S LITTLE SISTER: My sister wanted to take her doll. [*To her father*] She wanted . . . to take her doll.

THE INHERITOR'S FATHER: But my father would have none of it.

THE INHERITOR'S LITTLE SISTER: My sister started crying and whining about it.

THE INHERITOR'S FATHER: But my father slapped her and told her: "Now you know why you're crying, crybaby."

THE INHERITOR: My sister is a crybaby.

THE INHERITOR'S FATHER: Who is asking you? My father is strict.

THE INHERITOR: That's why therefore I was hiding my slingshot, right?

THE INHERITOR'S FATHER: Wrong, rephrase.

THE INHERITOR: So this is why I hid my slingshot.

THE INHERITOR'S FATHER: You don't say: "That's why therefore" . . . You say: "Therefore, I hid" . . . or better still, "And that is why I hid . . ." Now that you mention it, give me that slingshot you're hiding—it's confiscated.

THE INHERITOR: And we left for what would be the greatest day of our vacation. We got into Daddy's beautiful car.

[*Everyone gets up on the bed and pretends to be the passengers in a car.*]

We sped along the main road that runs along the river and which was slightly wet and slippery because of the rain that kept falling and . . .

THE INHERITOR'S MOTHER: Careful! Don't get carried away with that slippery road.

What about some punctuation?
It's chilly.

THE INHERITOR'S LITTLE SISTER: We're freezing.

THE INHERITOR: It's chilly. We're freezing.

[*Sudden braking.*]

THE INHERITOR'S FATHER: Don't repeat your sister's words. In an
essay, you just write "it's cold, period." My father informed us
that he wanted to educate and entertain us: "It's for this very
reason," he said, "that we are going to have a picnic in the Louvre
Museum."

THE INHERITOR'S MOTHER: "What a wonderful idea," said my mother,
who loves having picnics in museums.

THE INHERITOR: So, we entered the big galleries of the museum. After
looking for a quiet little spot, we laid out our picnic blanket in the
Impressionists' room.

THE INHERITOR'S MOTHER: Ah! What a delightful chiaroscuro!

THE INHERITOR'S FATHER: I parked in the perspective.

THE INHERITOR'S LITTLE SISTER: Oh! Mom, there's a lady swimming
totally naked.

THE INHERITOR'S MOTHER: Oh! Oh! Oh! Come here! You can't even
have a little peace and quiet in public places anymore. My mother
always thought there was nothing better than the Impressionists for a picnic. Listen, you speak very poorly; say instead, "My
mother always thought the Impressionists were best suited
for a luncheon on the grass. Pissarro, Manet, Monet, open air
painting."

THE INHERITOR'S FATHER: Take in the fresh air, my children, breathe . . .

THE INHERITOR'S LITTLE SISTER: My sister wanted to pick one of Monet's water lilies.

THE INHERITOR'S FATHER: But my father would have none of it, telling her that nature must be respected, and "water lily" is spelled with a y and not two i's, you idiot.

THE INHERITOR'S LITTLE SISTER: "And let's stuff ourselves!" shouted my sister, who got hell for not saying "Lunch is ready," as you should.

THE INHERITOR: After we have sat.
[*They get up.*]
After we were seated.
[*They get up again.*]
After sitting
[*They sit down.*]
in the shade, we heartily ate Mom's cooking.

THE INHERITOR'S FATHER [*with a full mouth*]: Bon appétit, with two p's.

THE PARK RANGER [*entering with an old record player in his arms*]: Bon appétit, ladies and gentlemen.

THE INHERITOR'S MOTHER: Thank you, Mr. Park Ranger.

THE INHERITOR'S LITTLE SISTER: Ah! Shit! He's going to ruin our best vacation.

THE INHERITOR'S FATHER: Mr. Park Ranger?

THE PARK RANGER: Sir?

THE INHERITOR'S FATHER [*handing him a record*]: Mr. Park Ranger, what do you think of Armand's homework?

THE PARK RANGER [*placing the record with the voice of Armand on the record player*]: Let's see, let's take a listen.

[*During this time, the characters mime at accelerated speed the actions performed earlier at normal speed.*]

THE RECORD: School was out. When I woke up in the morning, I felt quite happy. We were going to have one of the greatest vacation days we've ever had.

THE PARK RANGER: I gave this seemingly banal assignment to invite our students to reflect upon beauty, time, and freedom.

THE RECORD: My father had long ago made the decision to take us on a picnic, if I may say so. Mother had prepared a big basket full of treats for us to enjoy.

THE PARK RANGER: Pay attention.

THE RECORD: My sister wanted to take her doll.

THE PARK RANGER: Doll. Two l's.

THE RECORD: But my father would have none of it.

THE PARK RANGER: Off topic.

THE RECORD: My sister started crying and whining about it. But my father slapped her and told her: "Now you know why you're crying, crybaby."

THE PARK RANGER: Ah! Neologism, neologism, neologism. Do not make use of such neologisms. I'm fining you.

THE INHERITOR'S FATHER: I apologize, Mr. Park Ranger! When this little one irritates me I can no longer control what I say!

THE PARK RANGER: I'm fining you.

THE INHERITOR'S FATHER: Mr. Park Ranger . . . !

THE PARK RANGER: I'm fining you.

THE INHERITOR'S FATHER: For one word.

THE PARK RANGER: One word! One word! But a word is a word, sir, it is a word!

THE INHERITOR'S FATHER: Just a word!

THE PARK RANGER: Always choose your words! One word and the balance tilts, one word and the vase overflows! It takes one word to laugh and one word to cry. A plebian word, a patrician word, a proper word, a dirty word, a cowardly word never comes back! Above all the key word, the last word, the word of condemnation or acquittal. One word, sir, it's yes or no. No one is supposed to ignore the word. I'm fining you!

THE INHERITOR'S FATHER: Mr. Park Ranger!

THE PARK RANGER: On guard!

THE INHERITOR: En garde to you!

THE PARK RANGER: Gar . . . banzo!

THE INHERITOR: Gar . . . goyle!

THE PARK RANGER: Gar . . . lic sauce!

THE INHERITOR: Gar . . . bage chute!

THE PARK RANGER: Gar . . . gler!

THE INHERITOR: Gar . . . nishing!

THE PARK RANGER: Gar . . . denia!

THE INHERITOR: Gar . . . ga . . . garroter!

[THE PARK RANGER *collapses.*]

THE PARK RANGER: OK, you have the final word!

THE INHERITOR'S LITTLE SISTER: Well done, you got him!

THE RECORD: We had the best vacation, thanks to Mom and Dad.

[*This line is repeated five times.*]

THE INHERITOR'S FATHER [*to* THE INHERITOR'S LITTLE SISTER]: You'd do well to imitate your brother.

THE INHERITOR'S MOTHER: He gives us nothing but satisfaction, that one.

[THE INHERITOR'S LITTLE SISTER *exits.*]

THE INHERITOR'S FATHER [*to* THE INHERITOR]: My dear child, you are now brilliant enough to pursue an education. Do you think he'll have the courage to leave us? Come on! Student life isn't so bad. We've all been there, what a good time, though: the Bohemian girls and the wandering mind. The poet's little garret looking out on the Seine, the sweeping conversations that float around and up like wafts of smoke . . .

THE INHERITOR'S MOTHER: If you ever need money, let us know.

THE INHERITOR'S FATHER: We're here for you.

THE INHERITOR'S MOTHER: Avoid promiscuity. Don't engage in too much politics.

THE INHERITOR'S FATHER: Let him live his life, the lucky devil! I wish I could take his place.

THE INHERITOR'S MOTHER: You know, one never works as well as when alone.

THE INHERITOR'S FATHER: You'll never have enough fun, serious as you are!

THE INHERITOR'S MOTHER: We are proud of you. Don't forget to take your sheets when you go.

THE INHERITOR'S FATHER: We'll pay you a visit, from time to time, in your bachelor pad.

THE INHERITOR: Leave me alone! I beg you: leave me alone. I can feel myself becoming a student.

THE INHERITOR'S FATHER: I understand you so well!

THE INHERITOR: You've never understood me. I need the absolute, yet you offer me nothing but cultural constraints. I hunger for originality, you crush me with your conventionality. I yearn for a life in the avant-garde, yet you surround me with petit bourgeois relics.

THE INHERITOR'S MOTHER: My dear child!

THE INHERITOR'S FATHER: He has to live with his time. At his age, I almost became a surrealist.

THE INHERITOR: I have to leave.

THE INHERITOR'S FATHER: A bad temper, but a strong character . . .

THE INHERITOR'S MOTHER: He'll understand later.

THE INHERITOR: I renounce you.

THE INHERITOR'S FATHER: I truly see myself in him. He really takes after me.

THE INHERITOR'S MOTHER: It's an ungrateful age! Ungrateful!

THE INHERITOR: Thanks, bye!

THE INHERITOR'S MOTHER: Kids will be kids.

THE INHERITOR'S FATHER: You will be a man, my son!

THE INHERITOR: Alone at last! Freedom, oh, what crimes should be committed in your name! Families, I hate you. Free at last from domestic colonization! I am now off to my university adventure, unshackled.

[*The guardian angel parents tuck in their little child "who must leave to go to the Sorbonne" but who, for now, stays snuggled up in bed.*]

THE INHERITOR'S MOTHER [*singing*]:
Your guardian angel, my darling
Your guardian angel, my dear
Invisible and close
Will protect you from foes.
He will watch over you, my dear
Never, no, never
Is anyone ever alone at all
Until they're dressed for burial
Your guardian angel, my dear
Will have you under his sway
You won't see a thing, my dear
You will obey
Always, yes, always
Your head you will lay
On the same pillow every day.

[THE INHERITOR'S MOTHER *and* THE INHERITOR'S FATHER *exit.*]

THE INHERITOR: Alone at last! No more domestic annoyances and petty school hassles. Now I'm going to immerse myself alone in a sea of intelligence and find partners to share their solitary games . . .
[*Silence.*]
I'm going to feel solidarity.
Alone at last! I am breathing the Sorbonne air!

THE NON-INHERITOR: What do you mean? Alone? I'm right here!

THE INHERITOR: Sorry, my good old friend! I'd completely forgotten about you.

THE NON-INHERITOR: I guess you've forgotten about the exam too?

THE INHERITOR: Oh, the exam, we'll see about that later!

THE NON-INHERITOR: But we're taking it in less than an hour.

THE INHERITOR: One hour in the life of a student, we can take it easy.

THE NON-INHERITOR: I wish it was over and done with.

THE INHERITOR: As for me, I wish it had started already! Come on, let's go find the others at the cafeteria.

[*The* CHORUS OF INHERITORS *in the background. A Salvation Army* LUNCH LADY, *ringing a bell, sings.*]

THE LUNCH LADY:
Stuff yourselves,
We'll do the rest.
[THE STUDENTS *kneel.*]
Get drunk,
We'll take care of you.

[*Start of* THE STUDENTS' *sprint. They each take a white tray and mime getting a student cafeteria meal.* THE INHERITOR *and* THE NON-INHERITOR *are at the end of the line. They stand apart from one another. They don't talk to one another.*]

THE INHERITOR: You think that's good?

THE NON-INHERITOR: There's a lot of it.

THE INHERITOR: We don't really have a choice.

THE NON-INHERITOR: That sounds like a reproach.

THE INHERITOR. You really like it, huh?

THE NON-INHERITOR. No . . . I'm in a hurry to finish it, to go cram for the exam.

[THE NON-INHERITOR *hurries toward his table.*]

THE INHERITOR: Cram!! Listen to this: cram! His lordship is grimly shutting himself up in his study to cram for the exam! His lordship is sitting down heavily in his chair. His lordship is assuming the posture of Rodin's Thinker, his eyes rolled backward. His lordship is bending backward: Beware! So there! Voilà! That's it. Poor results for an afternoon of cramming.

THE NON-INHERITOR: Leave me alone, I have work to do.

THE INHERITOR: Keep it down: they might hear us.

THE NON-INHERITOR: Obviously, I have work to do. Everybody works.

THE INHERITOR: There's work, and there's work.

THE NON-INHERITOR: I don't really see the difference.

THE INHERITOR: So how do you explain that people envy students so much?

THE NON-INHERITOR. There's no reason to because studying is no picnic.

THE INHERITOR: Studying?

THE NON-INHERITOR: Isn't that what students do?

THE INHERITOR: What? No! You're playing with words. Students don't study. Come on, does an applicant apply? To shape the mind, you first have to be in shape. Shape before all. Breathe deeply.

[THE NON-INHERITOR *tries as best he can to follow* THE INHERITOR'*s injunctions.* THE CHORUS OF INHERITORS, *playing "*THE STUDENTS*" follows them easily.*]

Exhale, release tension. One, two, breathe in. One, two, breathe out.
　　Smile. Release tension. Look smart. Repeat: "I am the best. I am
　　the best."

THE NON-INHERITOR: I am average, I am average.

THE INHERITOR: No! Breathe in, repeat: the best, the best, the best.

THE NON-INHERITOR: I can't do it. I'm trying, though. Listen, leave
　　me alone, I have work to do, I have an exam.

THE INHERITOR: But so do I, my dear old friend, I have an exam too.
　　But be reasonable, the night is young.

THE NON-INHERITOR: Let me work, let me work.

[THE NON-INHERITOR *returns to his table. Burst of laughter from all the students. They approach* THE INHERITOR'*s table and start dancing in a circle around this table, threatening and light-hearted at the same time.*]

THE STUDENTS [*childish nursery rhyme*]:
He confesses, he confesses
He crams, he crams
He cheats, he cheats
He doesn't know how to play like us
He confesses, he confesses
He crams, he crams
the crammer, the cheater
[*Low and menacing*] We'll show this little traitor.
We'll tar him sooner or later.

THE NON-INHERITOR: Leave me the fuck alone! I want my spot!

THE STUDENTS [*lifting* THE NON-INHERITOR's *table over his head*]:
[*Rhythmically*]
If he works himself to death
The little traitor
It's not to put bread on the table
It's for the cash
If he gets up early
If he goes to bed late
It's to put frosting on the cake
On the table
One, two, three
[THE STUDENTS *let the table fall on* THE NON-INHERITOR's *head.*]
[THE STUDENTS *repeat the children's nursery rhyme from the beginning, ending this time with:*]
The little traitor

THE INHERITOR: Calm down, my friends! We must excuse him. He's hopped up by doping and dumbed down by revisions. We must help him have fun. We must explain to him what student life is all about.

FIRST STUDENT: First, a student has all his time, even that of others. He's free all week, but he is busy on Sundays.

THE STUDENTS [*with admiration*]: On Sundays!

FIRST STUDENT. Or the reverse, because being a student is a full-time job.

THE STUDENTS: Ah!

FIRST STUDENT: But that full time can be empty.

THE STUDENTS: Empty!

FIRST STUDENT: It's an elastic time!

THE STUDENTS: Elastic time!

SECOND STUDENT: Second, a student doesn't study. But he doesn't have fun either. If he has to, he stays up all night. If he doesn't want to, he doesn't get up.

THE STUDENTS: He doesn't?

SECOND STUDENT: He has every choice at his fingertips: he can find leisure in his labor or labor in his leisure.

THE STUDENTS: Leisure!

SECOND STUDENT: His freedom is his work—his work is his freedom!

THE STUDENTS: Freedom?

SECOND STUDENT: It's an eclectic time.

THE STUDENTS: Eclectic time?

THIRD STUDENT: Third, a student's life is short. It's a supercharged life. He doesn't know the double life of the civil servant, inscrutable at his desk, a passionate lover in bed. No! A student can read in bed as well as make love upon his desk. It's an electric time.

THE INHERITOR: Eclectic, elastic, electric. He has three times more time than the others.

THE STUDENTS [*slowly returning each to their places at the university cafeteria*]: Three times more time, three times more time, three times more time.

THE INHERITOR: You needn't panic. There's time for everything. We've had a laugh. Now, to work. Day merges with night. Time electrically unwinds, stealing news from the already future minutes of the dream. Everyone to work, everyone to the movies.

[*In the strobe light,* THE STUDENTS *excitedly shake their cafeteria trays. Each* STUDENT *wields a cafeteria tray like a small screen.*]

FIRST STUDENT: A brilliant anamorphic contribution to Expressionism.

SECOND STUDENT: Look! A very Baroque assault!

THIRD STUDENT: Give us some action!

FOURTH STUDENT: Ah! I love Westerns and genocides!

FIFTH STUDENT: Ah! No! A deceitful tracking shot to represent pederasty!

SIXTH STUDENT: Love through a telephoto lens.

SEVENTH STUDENT: An absurd interpretation of the structure of vampirism.

EIGHTH STUDENT: We cinemaniacs want a natural camera.

NINTH STUDENT: A VistaVision, Super Technirama 70 mm camera.

THE NON-INHERITOR: Bravo!

THE STUDENTS: Hush!

THE NON-INHERITOR: Go on! Waste your time!

THE STUDENTS:
Quiet! Let us work! Quiet!
Let us talk! Quiet!

THE NON-INHERITOR: I shouldn't have stayed, I'd have been better off working.

EIGHTH STUDENT: Out!

SECOND STUDENT: You're jealous.

SIXTH STUDENT: Out!

NINTH STUDENT: You're a nuisance!

SEVENTH STUDENT: Out!

THIRD STUDENT: You're a spoilsport!

FIFTH STUDENT: You're a killjoy!

ALL: Out!

THE NON-INHERITOR: Stop your reels! I can't hear myself think. I want to study.

[THE STUDENTS *retreat*.]

NINTH STUDENT: He takes food from our mouths.

FOURTH STUDENT: He wants us to die of hunger.

SEVENTH STUDENT: Let's kick out the traitor!

THIRD STUDENT: Let's get rid of the cockroach!

NINTH STUDENT: You will pay, sooner or later.

FIFTH STUDENT: We'll take you out like a dog, in-self-de-fense.

SEVENTH STUDENT:
Listen, you dregs of the Republic
Victory goes
To the intelligent ones
Who open the ghettos

ALL: With caution.

SEVENTH STUDENT: And sew on the yellow star.

ALL: Without being blamed.

[THE STUDENTS *go out*.]

THE INHERITOR: Enough with the studying already! Let's go to class and have some fun.

THE NON-INHERITOR: But I already have the notes.

FIRST PROCTOR: Program! Program!

THE INHERITOR: Seriously, there's no way I can take the exam without showing my face at least once.

THE NON-INHERITOR: Listen! Go ahead if you want. As for me, I have to reread my notes.

THE INHERITOR: It's too late to reread your notes.

THE NON-INHERITOR: It's never too late.

THE INHERITOR: We've got to see this . . .

FIRST PROCTOR: Program!

THE INHERITOR: This show is amazing. Very well. I'll go by myself, then.

[THE STUDENTS *enter.*]

THE NON-INHERITOR: No, wait for me!

[*All sit at the foot of the bed, which serves as a platform. On the bed, a box serves as a podium.*]

SECOND PROCTOR: Program! Program!
Ladies and gentlemen, the Sorbonne is happy to welcome such a large crowd. Those who don't have a seat can sit on the radiators. Ladies and gentlemen, it is an honor that this event should feature the man who makes you see and think. Performing here, one night only, the illusionist who remains clear even in mystery, the master of spiritualism, the hypnotist of crowds, the big shot who revives the dead. Ladies and gentlemen, I give you Professor Magus.

THE STUDENTS: Ah! Oh!

[SECOND BIRD-PROFESSOR *enters.*]

THE NON-INHERITOR: Do you think it's part of the syllabus?

THE INHERITOR: Who cares? It's for the love of art.

SECOND BIRD-PROFESSOR: Ladies—ladies and gentlemen, we are going to stop and linger a bit on the Knight of Espine. The Knight of Espine, the man and the work. If you allow me, ladies and gentlemen, our first talks will be about the man, and the last ones about the work. Now, the man. Then, the work!

THE STUDENTS: First part.

SECOND BIRD-PROFESSOR: Our enterprise will stay within the limits of modesty. It will be a complete resurrection of the past. We will bring the body of the Knight back to life right before your very eyes, and as an extension of this class, we will then evoke his spirit.

THE STUDENTS: Part One, heading A, heading B.

SECOND BIRD-PROFESSOR: For the sake of clarity, I'll cut the man into several pieces. Today the head, tomorrow morning, the heart, and in three days at the same time, then the lower stomach. I will deliberately leave out whole pieces of our program, like the legs, for example: they would take us too far.

THE STUDENTS [*bordering on heckling*]: Subheading A, the head; subheading B, the heart; subheading C, the lower stomach.

THE INHERITOR: Subheading A, subheading B, subheading C . . . Who does he think we are? It's too clear, it's too basic! We want our money back!

THE STUDENTS: Money back! Money back! Too basic! Too basic! Money back!

SECOND BIRD-PROFESSOR [*aside*]: Tough crowd today, I'm going to warm up the room. [*Loudly*] Ladies and gentlemen, I understand you very well, and I'm going to show you subheading A: the head. *Hic et nunc surgeat caput equitis Spinae per pulverem perlinpimpinam.*

[*The head of* THE KNIGHT OF ESPINE *appears at the podium.*]

THE STUDENTS: Ooh! Ahh!

THE NON-INHERITOR: I didn't get that, how did he do it?

THE INHERITOR: Watch instead of taking notes.

THE STUDENTS: Quiet! Who cares? Don't disturb the séance.

SECOND BIRD-PROFESSOR: Let us critique, critique this head in order to infer its intrinsic meaning from its essential form.

THE INHERITOR: Listen up! It's getting better.

SECOND BIRD-PROFESSOR: The hair: flat and brown. This observation is undermined by historical documentation which informs us that he wore a wig that was, I quote, "blond and frizzy." The duality of the head, the duality of the work. The bleak banality of it all concealed behind a baroque mask. The eyes: brown and farsighted, as you know from the famous sonnet: "Your eye, O Knight, sparkles and lights up. . . . " The impressionistic quality of the work that does a bad job of matching color and objects and of connecting form and content. The nose: straight. Expressing the righteousness of his literary instinct and balanced inspiration. The mouth: a means of communication—the work is dialogue.

THE STUDENTS: Hair: baroque; eyes: impressionist; nose: inspiration; mouth: communication.

THE INHERITOR: Let's speed up the schedule. Let's evoke the spirit of the Knight. *Hic et nunc surgeant anima et animus equitis Spinae per operationem spiritus sancti.*

[THE KNIGHT OF ESPINE's *head comes alive.*]

THE STUDENTS: Oh! Oh!

THE NON-INHERITOR: I don't get it—how'd he do it?

A STUDENT: Quiet!

ANOTHER STUDENT: Don't disturb the séance.

THE STUDENTS: Take note, take note of this wonder in silence.

THE NON-INHERITOR: Excuse me, sir?

THE INHERITOR: Are you out of your mind?

THE STUDENTS: Quiet!

THE NON-INHERITOR: Sir? I'm sorry, I didn't really understand—

SECOND BIRD-PROFESSOR: I am glad to hear this question which I have been expecting. [*Aside*] Now for the heavy artillery. [*Loudly*] I like it when students demonstrate critical thinking . . . Now you're feeling sleepy . . . It's the sign of an alert intelligence . . . Your head is heavy . . . Here's my answer in all honesty . . . A heavy sleep . . . It's about a common phenomenon . . . You feel a strange fluid . . . of metempirical transmission . . . I am putting a spell on you . . . about the epiphenomena . . . I am fascinating you . . . of the spirit's spirituality . . . You are sleeping . . . Sleep! Do you understand now? It's perfect. Let's move on.

[THE STUDENTS *are all hypnotized.*]

THE KNIGHT OF ESPINE: No, I didn't get it.

SECOND BIRD-PROFESSOR: Oh stop! It's a bit much. I am the one doing the talking here, not you. I am the professor. You're only one author on the syllabus. Just face the facts.

THE KNIGHT OF ESPINE: Not only did you cut off my head, you're also cutting me off.

SECOND BIRD-PROFESSOR: But you've already said it all! I'm repeating what you've said. The students repeat what I say about what you said. So, I'm begging you, say no more.

THE KNIGHT OF ESPINE: I still don't get it.

SECOND BIRD-PROFESSOR [*to* THE STUDENTS]: Wake up! Wake up! And now, ladies and gentlemen, another number for which I will need your collaboration. Gone is the gulf between the audience and the stage. Let's collaborate. I'm going to ask you questions. You're going to give me the answers. First question: What color are the Knight's eyes?

FIRST STUDENT: What is the pain of the horseman's games?

SECOND STUDENT: What is the value of the shoemaker's flames?

THIRD STUDENT: What is the wager of the friar's aims?

FOURTH STUDENT: What trimming leaves the tree in chains?

THE INHERITOR: Do you understand anything? It's so cool.

FIFTH STUDENT: Do you understand? You're going to fail, you fool.

SIXTH STUDENT: Do you compliment a square?

SEVENTH STUDENT: Are you completely unaware?

THE NON-INHERITOR: Your brain is completely filled with air!

SECOND BIRD-PROFESSOR: Thank you all. I'll conclude since you're making me feel I have to. Cursed are those who won't repeat. Cursed are those who will only repeat. Farewell, ladies, gentlemen. We'll see each other at the exam.

[*Flight of* THE STUDENTS *as* THE PROFESSOR *and* THE KNIGHT OF ES-PINE *laugh.*]

THE INHERITOR: You see, it's not hard. You just have to repeat without too much . . .

THE NON-INHERITOR: I see, but I didn't really get it.

THE INHERITOR: Let's go pay our respects.

THE NON-INHERITOR: You think we could ask him for some clarifications?

THE INHERITOR: But of course! [*To* THE PROFESSOR] Attending your class has taught me how to love.

SECOND BIRD-PROFESSOR: Teaching is a labor of love.

THE NON-INHERITOR: Excuse me, sir.

THE INHERITOR: You've introduced me to tenderness and beauty.

SECOND BIRD-PROFESSOR: My thesis cost me about thirty years of my youth.

THE NON-INHERITOR: Excuse me, sir!

THE INHERITOR: I felt the freshness of each and every written word.

SECOND BIRD-PROFESSOR: For you, child, I exhumed this manuscript.

THE NON-INHERITOR: Excuse me, sir!

THE INHERITOR: I tasted the harmony of each exotic group of lines.

SECOND BIRD-PROFESSOR: I re-counted the feet of the disyllabic rhymes.

THE INHERITOR: I do find originality exhilarating.

SECOND BIRD-PROFESSOR: From the original text, knowledge will spring. You were sitting in the front row when I saw you.

THE INHERITOR: In white linen, exuding ingenuous honesty, as I do.

THE NON-INHERITOR: Sir.

SECOND BIRD-PROFESSOR: I say: *Ex ore parvulorum veritas.*

THE INHERITOR: *Felix qui potuit rerum cognoscere causas.*

SECOND BIRD-PROFESSOR: *O fortunatos nimium sua si bona norint discipulos.*

THE NON-INHERITOR: Sir!

THE INHERITOR: *O sancta simplicitas.*

THE NON-INHERITOR: Sir, sir!

SECOND BIRD-PROFESSOR: *O tempora, o mores.*

THE NON-INHERITOR: Sir, sir!

THE INHERITOR: *Amen.*

THE NON-INHERITOR [*shouting*]: Excuse me, sir. I'm sorry, sir. I didn't really get it.

SECOND BIRD-PROFESSOR: I'm listening.

THE NON-INHERITOR [*pointing out* THE KNIGHT OF ESPINE]: I could be asked about this for the exam.

SECOND BIRD-PROFESSOR: Who knows? Fate works in mysterious ways. I must be off now. We're overwhelmed with work. Your classmate gets it. He'll explain it to you.

THE KNIGHT OF ESPINE: Professor, Professor, don't leave me behind!

THE INHERITOR: Just a minute, we'll take care of you. [*To* THE NON-INHERITOR] Don't you understand that all you have to do is know how to repeat?

THE NON-INHERITOR: Repeat what?

THE INHERITOR: Ask the Knight. He was privy to the Professor's private life for a long time. Weren't you, Knight?

THE KNIGHT OF ESPINE: I beseech you, sir! A little respect.

THE INHERITOR. Do not force me into violent acts I would regret. [*He tortures* THE KNIGHT OF ESPINE, *who howls.*] Come on! Spit it out, Knight! What does the old man expect from us?

THE KNIGHT OF ESPINE: What do you want me to tell you?

THE INHERITOR: Anything that will make our exegete happy.

THE KNIGHT OF ESPINE [*yelling*]: Don't hurt me! He loves a paradox: I wrote some very beautiful prose, but he only likes my wicked verses that, unfortunately, he discovered and edited . . .

THE INHERITOR [*torturing* THE KNIGHT OF ESPINE]: Anything else?

THE KNIGHT OF ESPINE: You needn't say more.

THE INHERITOR: It's not so hard, you see. You repeat this from memory back to the old man, looking candid, and your fortune is made.

[THE INHERITOR *and* THE NON-INHERITOR *carry off the box in which* THE KNIGHT OF ESPINE *is confined.*]

THE KNIGHT OF ESPINE: Gentlemen, please look after me! Gentlemen!

THE INHERITOR: Shut up! You've bothered us long enough!

THE KNIGHT OF ESPINE: Gentlemen!

THE INHERITOR: Quiet!

THE KNIGHT OF ESPINE: I could meet you at the exam.

THE NON-INHERITOR: Are you out of your mind? Did you hear him?

THE INHERITOR: Don't worry! You never get these on an exam. It's always the others, the old ones.

[THE NON-INHERITOR *returns to his table and picks up his notes.*]

THE NON-INHERITOR: Quick! Hurry up! We're going to be late.

THE INHERITOR: Easy, easy.

THE NON-INHERITOR: But hurry up, they'll be taking attendance.

[*Enter* THE STUDENTS *distributing fliers.*]

THE NON-INHERITOR: Go away please.

FIRST STUDENT: Comrade, get involved!

THE NON-INHERITOR: Quick! Get out of here!

SECOND STUDENT: Enlist!

THIRD STUDENT: Join!

FOURTH STUDENT: Support!

THE NON-INHERITOR: Leave! I'm taking my exam!

FIFTH STUDENT: Don't waste your time! There may not be an exam.

THE NON-INHERITOR: There are always exams!

SECOND STUDENT: Except when comrades decide to boycott them!

THE NON-INHERITOR: You can't do that!

SIXTH STUDENT: Quiet! This is a respectable place.

SEVENTH STUDENT [*on the stairs behind the bed*]: No more exams! Let us never be questioned again, never be tortured again! Culture is a crazy gesture, a loving embrace, a brandished gun. We do not punch the clock for culture! No more control and controllers! No more gates that separate, corridors that divide! Let us all vote now for a General Exam Strike.

[THE STUDENTS *throw their fliers in the air by the hundreds.*]

THE NON-INHERITOR: Wait!

SEVENTH STUDENT: Long live freedom!

THE NON-INHERITOR: Wait until my exam is finished!

FIRST STUDENT: Don't you get it at all? No more exams!

THE NON-INHERITOR: It can't be! This can't be real!

FOURTH STUDENT: It is real by unanimous consent.

THE NON-INHERITOR: You're not abiding by the rules.

SEVENTH STUDENT: This is majority rule.

THE NON-INHERITOR: Come on now! Explain it to them! Tell them you're against it!

THE INHERITOR: Come on! Show them you're a man.

THE NON-INHERITOR: Listen! I'm against it! That's enough! You're all out of your minds! You're acting against your own interests! If that's what you want—fine. But don't drag everyone else down with you.

SEVENTH STUDENT: Wait before speaking! Are you asking for the floor?

THE NON-INHERITOR: The floor! I'm not into politics.

SEVENTH STUDENT: The speaker has the floor.

THE NON-INHERITOR [*climbing up the stairs*]: I came here to take my exam, that's all. You might be strong enough to go forward without taking your exams, but I'm not.

SECOND STUDENT: Dirty little bourgeois! An insult is not an argument.

THE NON-INHERITOR: You're all talk, it's your right! But I'd rather have something tangible than all your big words. I want to take my exam.

SEVENTH STUDENT: You prefer a scrap of paper to the struggle of the workers.

THE NON-INHERITOR: Don't raise your hands to vote, comrades! Your soft hands will expose you!

SIXTH STUDENT: You are insulting a worker.

THE NON-INHERITOR: In short, you want to boycott luck. Because the exam is the first and last chance that I'm being given. A worker who is looking for work doesn't go on strike.

FOURTH STUDENT: The workers are inviting us to join them!

EIGHTH STUDENT: You're making a deal with the regime.

THE NON-INHERITOR: You're fascist collaborators disguised as resistance fighters. If they kick you out, you come back in through the window. I'll be tossed into the street.

THIRD STUDENT: Out on the streets to sell yourself for money.

THE NON-INHERITOR: You're daddies' boys! I'm not! I'm the son of whoever pays me to succeed. Without a scholarship, I'd be serving you!

FIFTH STUDENT: Sellout!

THE NON-INHERITOR: I only speak for myself. I can only speak for myself.

THE STUDENTS: A conformist from the lower middle class.

FIFTH STUDENT: You fill us with joy.

SECOND STUDENT: By showing us your ass.

NINTH STUDENT: Ambiguous.

EIGHTH STUDENT: Ill at ease.

SIXTH STUDENT: Sitting on the fence.

SEVENTH STUDENT: One buttock on your side.

FIFTH STUDENT: The other on the Establishment's.

THE STUDENTS [*circling around him until he falls on the bed*]: Crash! Bang! Crash! Bang!

THE INHERITOR: Comrades, comradeship between comrades does not aim to divide comrades. Let's elevate the debate. In dividing us, you're playing reactionary games. We need to lash out at the powers that be. They're our true enemies! We've had it with the old vulture, the petit bourgeois fowl. Professors, you are old and your culture is too.

[*Enter* THIRD BIRD-PROFESSOR *with a helmet and a police baton.*]

EIGHTH STUDENT: Plucked giblets!

THIRD STUDENT: Scrawny loser!

NINTH STUDENT: Toothless vampire!

FIRST STUDENT: Penguin!

TENTH STUDENT: Stork!

SECOND STUDENT: Sad cuckoo!

SEVENTH STUDENT: Hooting bird!

SIXTH STUDENT: Stinking bird!

FOURTH STUDENT: Droopy pecker!

FIFTH STUDENT: The only way is down!

THE INHERITOR:

So, we've shut you up, filthy owl!

You don't want to respond to us then? You talked too much earlier on!

We have something to say too. Are you deaf, old crow?

SEVENTH STUDENT: Long-winded magpie!

FIFTH STUDENT: Clucking starling!

TENTH STUDENT: Woodcock!

EIGHTH STUDENT: Rambling jay!

SIXTH STUDENT: Jabbering gander!

EIGHTH STUDENT: Paper hen!

TENTH STUDENT: Guinea fowl!

THE INHERITOR: He's making fun of us, the dirty nightingale! His lordship isn't coming down from his perch! He's dozing peacefully and leaving us in the bird shit!

THIRD STUDENT: Like a deep-fried whole chicken!

FOURTH STUDENT: Hammy turkey!

FIRST STUDENT: Overfed peacock!

NINTH STUDENT: Frigid crane!

FIFTH STUDENT: Braggart duck!

SEVENTH STUDENT: Prideful pheasant.

THE INHERITOR: I accuse you, old hen, of being sterile!

THIRD BIRD-PROFESSOR: *Tu quoque mi fili!* Now, now, children, recess is over. It's time for the exam.

CERTAIN STUDENTS: So be it!

[*They kneel; others do not.*]

THIRD BIRD-PROFESSOR [*pulling a police baton from behind his back*]: Recess is over! [*He bludgeons the remaining students, who fall to their knees like the others.*] Outside of school, no salvation. The school chooses the chosen.

[*Three times, like a shepherd guiding his flock, he exits.* THE STUDENTS *follow him, on all fours, like sheep.*]

THE NON-INHERITOR: After the exam, I'll get into politics. I'll fully commit myself. I'll tackle the root cause of the problems. I have a scholarship. All those who don't have one and who deserve one should have one too. Then everyone could succeed. Everyone would have the same chances.

THE INHERITOR: Yes, everyone would have the same chances.
[*Silence.*]
We are up now.
Let's get ready.

THE NON-INHERITOR: We knew it was coming.

THE INHERITOR: We laugh all night and then morning comes. There's no way around it.

THE NON-INHERITOR: You're not going to chicken out, right?

THE INHERITOR: I don't like to do that.

THE NON-INHERITOR: To think I almost skipped it.

THE INHERITOR: As if it was the only thing to worry about!

THE NON-INHERITOR: If you skip something, it will come back to haunt you.

THE INHERITOR: Don't you want to talk about something else?

THE NON-INHERITOR: I've never had any luck, and nothing's changed.

THE INHERITOR: Shut up, you're making me sick. I'm incapable of getting a word out.

THE NON-INHERITOR: You have to talk! You have to talk! That's all they like.

THE INHERITOR: Shut the fuck up! We'd do better to change the subject. Can you play poker?

THE NON-INHERITOR: No! . . . We can play solitaire!
[*He lays out the cards.*]
If I draw a red card, I pass my exam—If not . . .
Pitter, putter, hearts aflutter—here, there, one, two, three, not a care.
Pitter, putter, hearts aflutter—far, near, one, two, three, mother's here.

THE INHERITOR: Oh! The queen of hearts . . . There it is.

[THE USHER *enters.*]

THE USHER: Sirs, it's time. Are you made up?

THE NON-INHERITOR: Made up?

THE USHER: Here are two boxes of makeup. Hurry up. The youth of today don't know any of the rules. The exams are broadcast live, on television . . . a little more powder here . . . The university is definitely keeping up with progress. Exams are no longer trials behind closed doors. More powder! More powder! The camera doesn't lie. There's nothing more objective than the eye of the camera . . . We're starting . . . We're starting . . . places, everyone! You here [THE NON-INHERITOR, *stage right*], and you there [THE INHERITOR, *stage left*].

[*A powerful projection of light, representing the camera, hits the face of the candidate each time he responds to a question from the examiners on the jury.*]

THE NON-INHERITOR: Don't separate us! He came to take the exam in my place.

THE USHER: Everyone, take your seats.

THE NON-INHERITOR: He came to help me.

THE USHER: It is strictly forbidden to help one another.

THE NON-INHERITOR: But we came to take it together.

THE USHER: Together! [*Laughs*] You mean: one against the other.

THE NON-INHERITOR: Listen! Help me! You can't do this. Refuse.

THE INHERITOR: Of course I can! It's my exam too.

THE NON-INHERITOR: Help me. I have to pass.

THE INHERITOR: Sorry. I helped you for as long as I could. Now it's every man for himself.

THE NON-INHERITOR: You can't take the exam. You don't know anything. You didn't even study.

THE INHERITOR: We'll see!

THE NON-INHERITOR: Bastard!

THE USHER: Shake hands! Shake hands like brothers, swearing to fight according to the Olympic ideal of the Roman gladiators. Take your seats now.

[*The courtyard. Enter the* THREE BIRD-PROFESSORS, *who are members of the exam jury.*]

THE PRESIDENT OF THE JURY: We, President of the Jury, swear to judge the two adversaries with impartiality, objectivity, and lucidity. The questions drawn in the lottery will be strictly equal for the two candidates. May the best candidate win! And let our conscience be our guide!

FIRST ASSESSOR: First question: World knowledge.

SECOND ASSESSOR: First question: One egg. Thirty seconds.

FIRST ASSESSOR: Tell us the names of the gallinaceous birds. [*Indicating* THE INHERITOR] You first, sir!

SECOND ASSESSOR: Start the clock.

[*The stopwatch is triggered.*]

THE INHERITOR: First and foremost, there is the hen, which is the female of the rooster, which we shall also cite among the gallinaceous birds. The hen, which is an excellent breeder, unlike the rooster . . . as demonstrated by the proverb, "If you want some eggs, put up with the prattling of the hens."

FIRST ASSESSOR: Answer recorded.

SECOND ASSESSOR [*to* THE NON-INHERITOR]: Your turn, sir!

THE NON-INHERITOR: Pheasant, partridge, turkey, peacock, rooster, hen, chicken, Guinea hens, and marsh hens.

FIRST ASSESSOR: The answer is more comprehensive.

SECOND ASSESSOR: One egg to zero.

FIRST ASSESSOR: Second question: Translation and critical analysis.

SECOND ASSESSOR: Second question: Two eggs. Forty-five seconds.

FIRST ASSESSOR: Translate and comment on the song of the starling: "Frut trut trulipit pit tri tri trulitpit trut."

SECOND ASSESSOR: Start the clock.

THE NON-INHERITOR: In a word, "Trut, trut": Hop, hop! "Trulipit":
I am here. "Pit": Here. "Tritri": Joy, joy! "Trulipit": Here I am.
"Trut": Hop!

THE INHERITOR: "Trut, trut, trulitpit, tri tri trulipit trut": Yes, I jump
and jump with joy; here I am. My translation tries to convey
simultaneously the bouncing rhythm of the song and the power
of the alexandrine . . .

THE NON-INHERITOR: Here we have the very simple song of the
bouncing starling . . .

THE INHERITOR: The twelve-syllable original text is not lacking in
glee, as expressed by the repetition of the "I" and "U" sounds . . .

THE NON-INHERITOR: The bouncing starling . . .

THE INHERITOR: And by the numerous alliterations in the passage:
"tri . . . trat . . ."

THE NON-INHERITOR: Trulipit.

THE INHERITOR: The caesura signals a pause in the vocals, as if the
bird had stopped singing between two branches. We have here
the rural evocation of a rustic happiness; the starling's ability
to enjoy his way of living poetically, unlike Virgil's farmers:
"O fortunatos nimium, sua si bona norint, agricolas!"

THE NON-INHERITOR: There, that's it.

FIRST ASSESSOR: Cut.

[The light of the "camera" disappears. The stage plunges into
darkness.]

SECOND ASSESSOR: Deliberation.

[*Bird cries from members of the exam jury.*]

FIRST ASSESSOR: Lights.

[*Lights come back on.*]

SECOND ASSESSOR: Verdict.

THE PRESIDENT OF THE JURY: We have noted the exemplary precision of the first candidate's translation, but his uninspired commentary saddened us. In contrast, we appreciated the second candidate's elegant analysis, but his translation is a mess. We are giving them each the same grade.

SECOND ASSESSOR: Two eggs to one.

FIRST ASSESSOR: Third question: Parrots and finches.

SECOND ASSESSOR: Third question: Two eggs.

FIRST ASSESSOR: Recite for us the first two quatrains of Baudelaire's *The Albatross.*

THE INHERITOR [*"inspired" recitation*]: "Often, for sport, the crewmen catch albatrosses, vast sea birds that follow, lax travel companions, the ship gliding across the bitter deep."*

THE PRESIDENT OF THE JURY: How admirably sincere!

FIRST ASSESSOR: As accurate as a parrot and as charming as a finch!

SECOND ASSESSOR: This boy has class.

FIRST ASSESSOR: And grace!

---

* This is the first of two Baudelaire recitations. Both are from Charles Baudelaire, "L'Albatros / The Albatross," in *The Flowers of Evil: Dual-Language Edition,* trans. Anthony Mortimer (Surrey, Eng.: Alma Books, 2016), 14–15.

THE NON-INHERITOR [*"uninspired" recitation*]: "No sooner have they placed these airy kings upon the deck than, awkward and ashamed, the albatross let their great white wings drag pitifully beside them like oars."

THE PRESIDENT OF THE JURY: The textual accuracy earns the second candidate one small egg. The eloquence and emotion earn the first candidate two eggs.

SECOND PRESIDENT: Equal score: three to three.

THE PRESIDENT OF THE JURY: To decide between you two, we will ask you a supplemental ten-point question. Answer in all honesty! Why are you here?

[THE MOTHERS *of the two candidates enter and respond in their place.*]

THE NON-INHERITOR'S MOTHER: Why is he here? He was summoned. He came to take the exam, to answer the questions. He came . . . I can feel it, but I . . . can't find the words . . . He came, because if he fails, he will always remain the same. There, that's all.

THE INHERITOR'S MOTHER: This brave lady is right. Her son came here to be successful. It's only natural. I've felt so humble listening to her. If my child is successful, he won't become someone else. He'll remain as we have always known him, with all his faults and attributes, and yet with something more. He will have opened up and been enriched—thanks to you.

FIRST ASSESSOR: Cut.

SECOND ASSESSOR: Deliberation.

[*Bird cries.*]

FIRST ASSESSOR: Lights!

SECOND ASSESSOR: Verdict [*indicating* THE INHERITOR AND THE NON-INHERITOR, *respectively*]: 13 to 3.

THE PRESIDENT OF THE JURY [*to* THE INHERITOR]: We congratulate you.

THE INHERITOR: I wasn't expecting this. Thank you. I am so lucky.

FIRST ASSESSOR: Don't be modest. There's no such thing as luck.

SECOND ASSESSOR: It was obvious to me that thanks to your class standing, you have a natural aptitude for success.

THE INHERITOR: My friend here deserved to succeed as much as I did. He worked hard, you know!

THE PRESIDENT OF THE JURY: He lacks the je ne sais quoi that makes you superior to him.

THE INHERITOR: I understand.

THE PRESIDENT OF THE JURY [*to* THE NON-INHERITOR]: My friend, your courage illustrates the proud motto of William of Orange: "It is not enough to hope in order to act." A word of advice, however. In your case, it's not enough to persevere to succeed. Hope to see you again, sir.

THE INHERITOR: What will become of him?

THE PRESIDENT OF THE JURY: It's not our responsibility to know his fate. It's no longer for us to decide. In more ways than one, it's better to focus on you. You have a bright future ahead of you.

[*Enter* EIGHT ANCESTORS.]

THE SECOND ANCESTOR: No more laughing, my boy. It's time to think about work now.

THE INHERITOR: Good-bye, my last morning. Good-bye, my last night. Goodbye, minutes of freedom. You slipped away without further ado, without a word. Why has my time come? I didn't harm anyone. Goodbye, bed. It's time to pack up, to leave this room. Farewell. I'll never forget.

[*He lies on the bed, motionless.*]

THE PRESIDENT OF THE JURY: Ladies and gentlemen, we salute the remains of a student who chose us as role models. In a crushing world, he has managed to achieve exemplary lightness. Yes, truth comes out of this child's mouth. We will therefore welcome him as an equal, with the honors he deserves. My child, we accept you as one of us.

THE INHERITOR [*singing*]:
I am the phoenix
[*Standing up on the bed, wearing the bird mask and toga of* THE PROFESSORS]
I am the rare bird
That you meet in every corner of the woods
I sing and I die
In order to sing again
With a stronger voice
[*Indicating* THE NON-INHERITOR]
You will never be reborn from your ashes
Clever parrot
Because you don't know how to sing
Like the phoenix
You're nothing but a hardworking woodpecker
Who pecks at the tree
But can't uproot it
I am the rare bird
That you meet in every corner of the woods

[*The alarm clock from the beginning of the play begins to sound. The actor playing* THE INHERITOR *comes downstage and says:*]

Thus ends our comedy
Night of insomnia, night of wakefulness
If you applaud, you will be applauding injustice
Never say "good luck"
The dice are loaded
If you applaud, you are applauding injustice
We are all accomplices.